The Amazing Miss Laura

HILA COLMAN

SCHOLASTIC BOOK SERVICES
New York Toronto London Auckland Sydney Tokyo

ISBN 0-590-30006-7

Copyright © 1976 by Hila Colman. All rights reserved. This edition is published by Scholastic Book Services, a division of Scholastic Magazines, Inc., 50 West 44th Street, New York, New York 10036, by arrangement with William Morrow and Company, Inc.

12 11 10 9 8 7 6 5 4 3 2 1   9   9/7 0 1 2 3 4/8
Printed in the U.S.A.
06

The Amazing Miss Laura

One

The house was small and dark, as many New England farmhouses are. It was only when they were bought by the city people, who broke through the walls of the tiny rooms, opening them up with wings of glass and terraced patios, that people exclaimed, "What a beautiful old house!"

Josie Smyrski hated her father's — actually her grandfather's — house. It smelled. Not a romantic farmhouse smell of freshly baked bread and pies, but of pig's blood and oil, of her father's barn overalls, her grandfather's old-man smell. She hated oilcloth on the kitchen table, the large, old-fashioned coal stove with its tank for hot water (never enough), and she hated watching her grandfather eat his supper without his teeth. On this warm June evening, the kitchen seemed stuffier than ever.

"Why don't you use your false teeth?" Josie asked testily.

"Because they hurt. That damn-fool dentist don't know how to fit them right." Her grandfather took a piece of unchewable gristle out of his mouth and laid it on the side of his plate, much to Josie's disgust. "Your knives need sharpening, Lena," he said to his daughter-in-law, Josie's mother. "And don't be stingy with the vinegar on those hog jowls," he added. "When we used to make them. . . ."

Josie got up from the table. She didn't want to hear for the umpteenth time how her grandmother used to pickle pig's jowls or watch her mother handle the head of the pig, slaughtered the day before by her father under her grandfather's directions.

Josie felt particularly edgy that evening. The excitement of her high school graduation had been over a week ago, but staying home all week had gotten on her nerves. What was she going to do now? Her art teacher had said she would like to see her go to art school, but what was the use of that advice when there was no money for it?

"You going to walk away with all the prizes tonight?" her grandfather asked jovially.

"What good will it do me?" Josie demanded fiercely. "I won't be able to go to art school anyway." The local library was having an arts-and-crafts show, and tonight the prizes were to be awarded. While Josie had her heart set on winning a prize with one of the paintings she had submitted, the thought of it now only added to her frustration. She didn't think she was a genius, but art school would be a way out, a way to get away from home, somewhere to go.

"It's doing something well that counts," her mother said. "Look at your father, your grandfather, they take pride in their work. Don't forget your grandfather built this house with his own hands, and your father's made most all the furniture. They never went to school to learn."

"She's right," her father said, looking up from the

small table he was sanding. "What do you think, Pop? Think I should sand it down some more?"

The two men studied the table critically. "Yeah, I think it needs some more," her grandfather said.

Everything in the household was done under her grandfather's orders. How could Josie ever forget that the house was his, that he had built it with his own hands, and that the farm was his, and what was more, that nothing in any of it was to be changed. She was told that over and over again. "After I die you can do what you want," he often said, "but while I'm alive and living here, it's going to stay the way it is."

Josie thought her parents were silly to let him get away with it. "He's an old man. Why should we have to do everything he wants? He should give the house to Pop now anyway. What does he need it for anyway?" Josie would say when her grandfather talked that way.

"This house and the farm are all the old man has," her mother told her. "If we took this away from him he'd have nothing. He'd die. He built this house for his bride. Your father was born here. It's like a record of his whole life. If we changed it, it wouldn't be his anymore."

"What about you and Pop, your lives?" Josie wanted to know.

"We can live with it," her mother said.

He's a stubborn, bossy, old crank, Josie thought to herself, and guiltily she wished he would die. But the old man seemed as strong as an ox.

By a stroke of luck, her grandmother, before she died, had persuaded him to put in a bathroom to replace the old outhouse, and even that was old-fashioned now, too.

Josie's one ambition in life was to get out. But she had no money and she didn't know where to go. The Connecticut farm country had changed since she was born, seventeen years before. Many farms had been sold to city people, who turned the farmland into lawns and rock gardens, swimming pools and tennis courts, and filled the village store with their chatter of New York plays, art shows, and new novels. Josie loved to listen to them. Some of the old-timers resented the city folk, but Josie thought they brought excitement and elegance to the sleepy village. She liked to pretend that she was one of them, one of the young, pretty girls. She didn't like the old ladies, the widows and schoolteachers, who had come up to Jacob's Brook to retire. She found them boring, the ones who asked her what her name was and if she was still in school, as if it was any of their business or if they cared. She answered them politely, "I'm Josie Smyrski, and I'm just graduating from high school."

Those who had lived in town for a while would smile and say, "Oh, you must be old man Smyrski's granddaughter. How is your grandfather? A wonderful old man. . . ."

A wonderful pain in the neck, Josie would think. In her opinion old people should be put out to pasture like horses. Everybody would be better off.

Josie went outside and sat on the fence overlooking her grandfather's fields. His seventy-odd acres were a main source of anger to Josie. The old man's peasant mentality, as she called it, made him refuse to part with even a small parcel. With property selling for between five and ten thousand dollars an acre, they could be rich, and Josie spent many hours daydreaming about what they could do with the money. The so-called farm wasn't much of a farm anymore, because it didn't pay. They had some pigs and chickens, a few cows for milk, and occasionally her father raised an Angus steer for beef. That plus a large vegetable garden and refinishing old furniture, her father's hobby, kept him busy. They wouldn't make out without her mother's factory job in the city, fifteen miles away. Her mother said they had nothing to complain of, because they had a roof over their heads and plenty of good food to eat. But Josie resented the fact that there was never enough cash to buy any of the wonderful things she saw in the stores, or now for art school.

The fields were pretty, but why the old man needed to hang onto all that land was more than she could understand. She could easily imagine few ranch-type houses on the lots by the road, and her grandfather wouldn't ever miss the ten or fifteen acres. She didn't believe him when he said he knew every blade of grass, and she was sure he was faking when he told her father, with explicit directions, what trees and bushes to prune and where they were. How could he remember all that when by the time supper came around he had forgotten what he had eaten for lunch?

"You'd be surprised," her father said. "He knows every inch of this property like the palm of his hand. You could make a map from what he tells you." Her father sometimes had fights with his father, and they yelled at each other at times, but Josie knew that her father was proud of the old man. She couldn't see what there was to be proud of. In fact, she thought her father was weak not to make his father step down, not to take over and give the orders, and especially not to sell off some of the land so that they could have the money.

Money was very much on Josie's mind these June days. Sooner or later she'd have to look for a job, but that too was a bleak prospect. There weren't many jobs around. Her mother thought she could probably get one at the factory, but to Josie that was a last resort. When she imagined going off to New York or Hartford to go to art school, she convinced herself that only money stood in her way, but she also knew she was scared. Home was dull but it was safe, and she wasn't sure she was that good. Still, she believed that if her father really wanted to, he could get the farm, or at least some of it, signed over to him so that he could sell it.

The last time a real-estate agent had come around to ask her grandfather if he wouldn't sell some land, she had had a big fight with him afterwards.

"What do you need it for? Nobody's using those fields or the woods. It's stupid to keep them when we could use the money. . . ."

"The money will be spent while the woods and fields stay here. In June there'll be fresh morels. Every June we used to eat them. Your grandmother knew how to fix them, best things you ever ate in your life. I don't need the money. What would I do with it? I'm happy living here, looking at my woods, my land. . . ."

"All you're thinking of is yourself. What about the rest of us? Mom wouldn't have to work in a factory — "

"Leave me out of this," her mother had cut in sharply. "I'm not complaining."

"Well, I am," Josie had yelled at them. "You're a bunch of sentimental idiots. Pigheaded Poles, that's

6

what you are. Times have changed. You don't care about me. I'm young; I want to live differently."

"Go ahead," her grandfather said, blowing his nose into a big red kerchief. "You live your life the way you want. You'll find money isn't everything."

"That's what you think. And don't worry, I'll live my life differently. You're damn right I will." Josie had stamped out of the house, but at the door she yelled back, "And it won't be the way you live either."

She had gotten no place except to deepen her own frustration and resentment. If the property were being used, she could see some sense to it. But there it was, not doing anyone any good, and she couldn't see the need to humor the stubborn old man when the money would mean so much to her, to the whole family. It wasn't as if he had to give it all up, just a few acres would do....

Josie wished she could stop thinking about it, but every time she looked out at the fields just sitting there, she got mad again.

Now Josie went inside and up to her room to brush her hair. She called down to her mother, "I'm going to the library. You want to come with me?"

"Yes, I'll come."

The two women side by side looked similar in their light cotton dresses, each with a cardigan thrown around her shoulders. While Josie took after her father's family, she had inherited her mother's sparkling brown eyes and wide Slavic face. Mrs. Smyrski was plump, but Josie was narrowly built and lean. There was no sidewalk from their house to the village, but the road they walked on was lined with trees and followed the gentle slope of the land. It wasn't much of a village: only one store, the post office, two churches on one side of the green, and the town hall, the small elementary school, the library, and the firehouse on the other.

Tonight the village was lit up more than usual, and the parking area in back of the library was full. The library itself was crowded with townspeople, most of whom Josie and her mother knew well.

Debbie, Josie's best friend, greeted them at the door. "Where were you? Come, look, you've got first prize! Aren't you thrilled?" Debbie grabbed Josie's arm and pulled her over to where her painting hung. And there it was, the first-prize blue ribbon stuck with a thumbtack alongside her painting. Josie stared at it in disbelief. Her painting! She remembered when she had done it: it had been in early spring, the first bright, sunny day after a spell of wet weather, a day fresh with the promise of languid summer days ahead. But it had not been a calm day for Josie. She had felt restless, left out, as if the burgeoning spring held something for everyone but her. Some of her mood had crept into her painting of the landscape of fields and a stream. While the use of her paints was not extraordinary, the picture had a sense of loneliness that set it apart from the others. Still, as Josie looked at it she could see a lot of things wrong with it, but what did it matter? Even if it were a terrific painting, it wouldn't get her anywhere.

Josie was hugged and kissed by her mother and congratulated by all her friends. She enjoyed being the center of attraction for the evening, but the feeling of frustration still nagged at her. Her art teacher asked her what she was planning to do. "I don't know if you have what it takes to be an artist," her teacher said, "but at least if you went to a good art school, even for a semester, you'd find out."

"It's not possible," Josie told her. She didn't want to talk about it, and she turned away.

On the walk home, her mother asked her the same question. "Josie, what are you planning to do?"

"What am I going to do, what I am going to do! Everyone's pestering me. I don't know what I'm going to do. Wait for Grandpa to die, that's what I'll do."

"Josie, don't you talk that way, even as a joke. Your grandfather worked hard all his life, and now he has a right to enjoy what years he has left, and his property is what he enjoys. You just forget about his fields."

"All right, all right, I'm sorry. But I don't know why you and Pop let him run everything. It beats me."

"Maybe we're content with the way we live. Besides, we love him," her mother added simply.

They walked the rest of the way home in silence. Josie felt ashamed of her outburst, especially when her father and grandfather made such a fuss about her winning first prize. "We're proud of you, Josie," her father said. "It runs in our family. Grandpa here used to do fine cabinetwork, and he taught me what I know, and I guess your painting ain't so different. Anything you can do by yourself with your hands will give you great satisfaction."

Some money would give me more satisfaction, Josie thought, but she kept her thoughts to herself.

Two

The next day Josie walked down to the village to meet her friends and to pick up her picture at the library. As usual, there was a group sitting on the grass on the green, some of them leaning up against the small plaque commemorating the local boys killed in the Second World War, Korea, and Vietnam. Josie joined her friends and lazily stretched out on the grass.

They were talking about their summer plans. Debbie was going to Maine with her parents to visit her grandparents, two of the girls had jobs as waitresses, one of the boys was going to be a lifeguard. . . . It seemed to Josie that everyone had plans except her.

"What are you going to do?" Debbie asked her.

"I'm sick of everyone asking me that. I don't know. Mope, I guess. Got any ideas?"

"Well, my mother's looking for someone to work for Mrs. Van Dyk over the summer while she's away. Mrs. Van Dyk wants a high school girl to stay with her. But you wouldn't want to live in, would you?"

10

Josie sat up. "Live in that house? I sure would. Anything to get out of my dump anyway."

"That old lady can be a terrible pain sometimes. My mother can tell you. I don't think my mother will go back in the fall, because the old lady needs someone to live in."

"All old people are a pain. But she's different, too — and that house! I was only in it once. It's beautiful."

Laura Van Dyk was the widow of a distinguished artist and lived in what Josie thought of as a mansion. The large, sprawling, white house set above the green on a knoll, surrounded by shade trees, was indeed the local showplace, with its five chimneys, French windows, and terraced formal gardens. Debbie's mother did what the village called "helping out" for Mrs. Van Dyk, which meant cooking and housecleaning. Paul Van Dyk, her artist husband, had been the village celebrity until his death a couple of years before, and his widow, now in her mid-eighties, had inherited the title. It was a sign of social acceptance to be invited to her house for dinner, and even now the writers and artists in the area treated her with a certain deference, though they might whisper behind her back that she was getting "befuddled." But Laura Van Dyk still walked with her head high, with the grace of a woman who had been beautiful all her life and accustomed to attention from all she came in contact with, from the grocer's boy to a visiting museum director.

Josie had long admired her from afar and could not put her in the class of "old people" with her grandfather. Mrs. Van Dyk never had spots on her stylish clothes, which were not the loose, ill-fitting things most of the other old women in town wore.

11

Earrings dangled from her ears, and sparkling rings adorned her fingers, and if she had false teeth, which Josie doubted, the fact was a tightly kept secret for herself alone. She was a glamorous, theatrical woman, and she gave Josie a glimpse into a world where everyone was rich and elegant and artistic.

"I couldn't do much cooking," Josie said.

"I don't think you'd have to. My mother arranged to have Mrs. Thompson come in a few times a week. Mostly Mrs. Van Dyk wants someone to drive her around, to keep her company more, and to sleep there at night."

"What do I do about it?"

"You really want to do it?" Debbie was surprised.

"Sure, why not? It's a job, and I'd rather spend the summer in her house than in ours."

Debbie nodded. "Yeah, but she's not easy. My mother says she's not all there."

"I'm used to that. At home I have to listen to my grandfather repeat himself a hundred times. With her at least I'd be getting paid."

"Why don't you call my mother now? She's over there. Maybe you could go over."

Josie didn't stop to think for long. She was ready to fasten onto anything that would get her out of her own house. And her mind was already spinning into the future. In a house like that maybe she'd learn something about painting, and she'd meet all kinds of interesting and artistic people, maybe someone who would take an interest in her, maybe get her a scholarship to an art school. . . .

Josie went across the street to the telephone booth next to the post office to make her call. When she was told that she could come for an interview then, she got nervous. She was wearing jeans and a T-shirt, but they were clean, so that was okay. And besides, that was what she wore most of the time, so she might as well be seen as she was. She stopped to comb her long, dark hair and peer into her pocket mirror to make sure her face looked all right. Not a bad face, an interesting face she was told, with high cheekbones, a small nose, and wide-set eyes that crinkled up when she laughed. A Slavic face, very much like that of her dead grandmother, who, she had been told over and over again, had been considered a beauty.

Josie walked up the flagstone path to the big house feeling shy. She had never come into close contact with anyone like Mrs. Van Dyk, and all her normal self-confidence fled, leaving her feeling like an unsophisticated farm girl, who would not know what to say or how to behave. She was tempted to turn around and go back — she didn't like feeling inferior — and settle for a job in the factory where she'd be with people she felt easy with, but her curiosity and her pride said no. Even though she came from a family of uneducated Polish farmers, she was as good as anyone, and if Mrs. Van Dyk didn't like her, to heck with it.

Mrs. Krupnik, Debbie's mother, greeted her at the door and led her into a small study where Mrs. Van Dyk was resting on a sofa and reading. Josie didn't dare look around the room, although she was aware of books lining the walls from floor to ceiling, of lots of plants in a large bay window, and of a beautiful fireplace outlined in blue-and-white tiles. Her eyes were on the woman on the sofa, her thick, almost-white hair piled high above her forehead, revealing sharp blue eyes deeply set in a lined, finely chiseled face, an aristocratic face that was now welcoming Josie with a cordial smile.

"Sit down, my dear." Mrs. Van Dyk put down her book and waved Josie to a chair. "Who are you? What's your name?"

"Josie Smyrski."

"I'm not going to try to remember your last name. I'll call you Josie. Tell me about yourself. How old are you? What have you been doing with your time?"

Josie got only as far as giving her age when Mrs. Van Dyk interrupted. "Ah, seventeen. A marvelous age! That was when I made my first trip abroad, the year before I came out. It was such a glorious summer, before the war — the First World War my dear, when we were going to save the world for democracy. Venice was beautiful in those days. I hear it's full of sewerage today. I'm glad I don't have to see it that way. . . ." Her voice trailed off, and she closed her eyes.

Josie sat watching her, not knowing what to do. She thought the old woman had fallen asleep, and she was afraid to move. But after a while Mrs. Van Dyk opened her eyes. "What did you say your last name was?"

Josie told her again.

"Smyrski, a good old Polish name. You are Polish, aren't you?"

"My grandparents came from Poland. I'm American I guess. I was born here, right here in Jacob's Brook."

"Were you really? How quaint. I suppose you're called a native. My husband always adored the natives — that's why he bought this house — but now the town is getting overrun with city people. They keep coming around and drinking up all my liquor. I ask them to tea, but nobody drinks tea anymore. It's always gin and tonic they want. I can hardly afford it...."

Josie didn't know how to get the conversation around to the job. The old woman's mind seemed to jump from one thing to another. She was getting worried when, after quite a long dissertation on the value of drinking tea, Mrs. Van Dyk suddenly asked, "Do you know how to drive a car?"

"Yes, ma'am. I've had a license since I was sixteen."

"Don't call me ma'am. I hate that word *ma'am*." She said it with disgust. "As a matter of fact, I think you can call me Miss Laura. Makes me feel young again. That's what the servants at home used to call me when I was a girl. Not that you're to think of yourself as a servant," she added quickly. "Servants have gone out of style, like everything else, and I am not an old-fashioned woman. I am very modern in my thinking." She was looking at her feet resting on a pillow on the sofa. "Do you like these shoes? I adore shoes. I once owned fifty-four pairs of shoes. Dear Paul — my husband, you know — counted them. He gave me quite a lecture about extravagance, but he didn't really mean it...."

Josie sat through another long, meandering tale, wondering if she would be there the rest of the day, when Mrs. Van Dyk sat up suddenly. "I'm talking too much. You must shut me up. That's one of your duties. I do not wish to make a fool of myself. When can you start to work for me?"

They arranged for Josie to move in the following Sunday and for her salary of sixty dollars a week,

15

which seemed like a lot of money to Josie, although she wasn't at all sure what her duties would be.

With a sigh of relief Josie left the house. Debbie was right, she decided. The old woman wasn't going to be easy, and she could be an awful bore, but Josie was already adding up all the money she would have at the end of the summer. And it was better than staying home. Also, she thought, she'd be able to figure out some way to avoid listening to Miss Laura's incessant chatter all day. "Poor, senile old thing," Josie said to herself. *Senile* was her word for almost anyone over sixty.

Josie walked home feeling quite pleased with herself. This morning she hadn't known what she was going to do with herself all summer, and now she had a job. She carried her painting under her arm, feeling that maybe her luck was turning: a first prize, and now a job with an artist's wife. The two things seemed to fit together, and even if the old lady was difficult, as she was sure to be, Josie was hopeful that somehow or other, if Mrs. Van Dyk took a fancy to her, she'd get some help in her art.

Josie announced her good news as soon as she got home. Her mother looked at her in astonishment. "How come you want to work for an old lady? I'd think that would be the last thing you'd want to do. You don't get along that good with your own grandfather."

"Well, she's different," Josie said.

"Having money don't make an old person any different," her father said bluntly. "If you last there a week, I'll be surprised."

"Thanks a lot for your encouragement. It's a job, sixty dollars a week, and I'll have my own room and bathroom — "

"You going to *live* there? Why can't you come home nights?" Mrs. Smyrski obviously did not like that idea.

"Because she wants someone to stay there, that's why. She doesn't want to be alone."

Her father chuckled. "Won't even last a week."

"I thought you two would be glad that I got a job so fast. I'm glad, if you're not, and I'll sure be glad to get out of here." Josie felt hurt and angry.

"Ain't such a bad house, Josie," her grandfather said from his corner rocker. "Ain't never been flooded, even in the hurricane of fifty-five. As good and sturdy a house as you'll ever find. But I remember that house that artist fellow bought — the old Hammett place. I put some cabinets in there, I guess forty years ago, maybe more than forty, can't remember. Maybe they're still there, beautiful cabinets made of the finest pine you could buy. You look for them."

"Yeah, yeah. . . ." Josie went up to her room and flung her picture down on her bed. She would be happy to get away, but her parents' words kept stinging. Maybe she was crazy to take a job living with a fussy, senile old lady. Yet it paid good money, and she had her own reasons for taking it. Mrs. Van Dyk wasn't someone ordinary; she had good connnections. Maybe something good could come of it for her.

Josie sat on her bed, looked at her painting, and tried to convince herself that she was doing the right thing, the smart thing, in spite of her parents' warnings.

Three

Josie stuck out her hand, turned off the alarm, and then pulled the sheet over her head. The early-morning sun was streaming in through the window, but she wanted more sleep. Ever since the end of school she had been sleeping until almost noon, but suddenly she remembered where she was. She was in a big, four-poster bed in Mrs. Van Dyk's house, not in her own narrow bed at home in a room that could barely hold the bed and a bureau under its low ceiling. This was her first day at work.

When she had brought her clothes over the day before, Sunday, Debbie's mother had been there to show her around, particularly in the kitchen, and to give her instructions. "Mrs. Van Dyk wants you to bring her a breakfast tray promptly at eight every morning. She has fruit juice, a toasted muffin, and coffee. One spoon of sugar and a little cream in the coffee. Right after her breakfast you're to go across to the post office and pick up her mail and her *New York Times*. This is absolutely routine, and if you bring that tray up later than eight, she'll let you know it. After that she'll tell you what she wants you to do. The days that Mrs. Thompson doesn't come in you can fix her a light lunch, a salad or a sandwich. Mrs. Thompson will take care of the dinners; she'll leave something you can just heat up when she's not here. She'll do the cleaning and take care of the laundry. Mrs. Van Dyk is very fussy about her cat. You must never let Heloise out of the house unless Mrs. Van Dyk is in the garden or you're out with her. If that cat ever gets lost, there'll be hell to pay."

What a pile of dull stuff to remember. None of it sounded too hard, but Josie felt nervous. She got up, washed herself quickly, and put on a shirt and a pair of shorts. She was on her way downstairs when Mrs. Van Dyk called out from her room. "Who's there?"

The old lady sure had sharp ears, because Josie didn't think her sneakers had made a sound on the carpeted steps. "It's me, Josie."

"Who are you?"

Josie went to the open door of the bedroom. Mrs. Van Dyk was sitting up in bed, her hair straggling loosely over her shoulders. She looked very old. "It's me, Josie, the girl who's working for you."

The old woman looked relieved. "Yes, of course. You'll have to forgive me, my dear. My memory's not what it used to be. I can remember what happened thirty years ago, but not what happened two hours ago. Are you bringing me my coffee? There's a blue-and-white cup I particularly favor. Paul always used to put a flower on my breakfast tray. Do you think you could do that? Something yellow would be pretty."

A flower, for heaven's sake! Old people and their

19

nutty ideas! Josie felt lost in the large kitchen. She had never seen so many dishes in her life. There were sets of dinnerware in the pantry, sets of dishes in the kitchen cabinets, and glasses and pots of every size and description. Josie had never imagined that anyone could own so many different kinds of dishes and kitchenware, but nowhere could she find a blue-and-white china cup and saucer. Had the old lady just imagined she owned such a thing? Was it something that had been broken thirty years before? As if it made any difference what color cup she used. Josie finally put a plain white cup and saucer on the tray with the coffeepot, juice, and muffin. Then she ran out into the garden and picked a yellow rose.

When she carried the tray upstairs, she was sure that Mrs. Van Dyk would have forgotten about the blue-and-white cup by now. But no sooner had she put the bed tray down in front of her than Miss Laura, as she again reminded Josie she wanted to be called, spoke sharply. "I said I wanted the blue-and-white cup. Where is it?"

"I couldn't find it," Josie apologized.

"Oh, that's my fault. I should have told you. It's on the third shelf over the dishwasher, in with the sugar and creamers."

Josie was sure now that Miss Laura had to be dreaming of long ago. When she brought the tray downstairs again, however, she took another look, and, sure enough, there was a blue-and-white cup exactly where the old woman had said it would be. The episode gave Josie a creepy feeling: a sense of not knowing where she was with Miss Laura. Debbie was right. That old lady certainly could be a pain. God help me, Josie thought, if she's going to check up on every detail. Just like her grandfather, Miss Laura was living in her own murky world of the past. Josie banged around the kitchen, wondering if she was out of her mind spending her summer with a nutty old woman, but she thought about the money she would have at the end of the summer and decided to stick it out. Besides, at home there was her grandfather, and he was just as impossible.

Josie's first week on her job was not an easy one. The house was gloomy, and after the first rays of the early-morning sun left, it was dark. At night the big house creaked with noises. Josie lay in bed with her lights on, terrified. There were rattling noises and scuttling noises, and she was sure she heard steps on the stairs. She was too frightened to get up to look and instead put her head under the covers and prayed.

The third night she was in the house there was a tremendous thunderstorm. Lightning flashed all around, and every time it thundered Josie held her hands over her ears under the covers. Suddenly, when there was one tremendous clap of thunder, all the lights went out. Josie felt she should go in to see how Miss Laura was, but she was too frightened to move. Then she was positive she heard steps on the stairs.

"Who's there?" she called out, afraid of the answer.

"It's me." Miss Laura's voice was clear.

Josie sat up in bed. "What are you doing?" The old lady certainly was crazy to walk around the house in the dark.

"I'm going to get some candles, of course."

Josie almost laughed. Timidly she got out of bed

and fumbled her way to the hall. In a flash of lightning she could see Miss Laura walking down the stairs in her nightgown. She didn't want to move, but she was afraid to let Miss Laura walk around the house in the dark. She felt her way down the steps, and there was Miss Laura calmy taking candles out of a chest of drawers, putting them into candle holders, and lighting them.

"Aren's you scared?" Josie asked in wonder.

"Of course not, child. You're safer here than anywhere. This house has stood for over a hundred years, and it's not about to be struck now. I've never been afraid of nature."

Josie couldn't believe that Miss Laura had known exactly where to find the candles. Only that morning Josie had spent hours trying to find the woman's glasses. She had been on her hands and knees under the bed; she had looked through her many pocketbooks; she had gone through the pockets of clothes hanging in the closet. She had looked in the kitchen and in the study, where Miss Laura had been reading the day before. Finally she had found the eyeglasses in a box of tissues next to Miss Laura's bed. "Of course," Miss Laura had said. "I remember now. I dropped them there when I answered the phone. My memory gets worse every day."

Josie had put the episode down to senility, especially when ten minutes later Miss Laura had misplaced her glasses again. And now there she was holding out a candle to Josie and taking two for herself. "One is for the bathroom," she said. "Be sure to blow your candle out when you get into bed. Don't fall asleep with it lit."

Josie felt foolish walking upstairs behind her boss.

She was supposed to be taking care of Miss Laura, but she felt right then that the roles were reversed.

Afterward Josie was more bewildered than ever. Was the old lady crazy or wasn't she? Josie didn't know what to expect from one minute to the next, and there was nothing in her background that prepared her to cope. At home she had paid as little attention as possible to her grandfather and had let her mother handle his forgetfulness and his demands.

The morning after the storm the sun shone brightly for what promised to be a perfect June day. When Josie brought up Miss Laura's breakfast tray, Miss Laura was sitting up in bed, her dark-blue eyes shining. "We're going to have a picnic today. I adore picnics. We'll have thin cucumber-and-watercress sandwiches and fresh strawberries and a bottle of wine. You can drink wine, can't you? In France babies drink wine, so it can't hurt you."

"Where will we go?" Josie could sense Miss Laura's excitement.

"Who knows? We'll go exploring, someplace we've never been to before. We'll sit on the grass and let the wine cool in the water. There'll have to be water. We don't have to have a destination. We'll just drive until we find a place we like. Won't it be fun?"

Josie wasn't exactly thrilled at the prospect of a picnic with Miss Laura, but she realized it was part of her job. Yet she couldn't help responding when Miss Laura got out of bed, strode to her closet, and flung open the door. "I'll wear a long skirt and a big hat the way I used to. Paul and I had marvelous picnics with our friends. Paul always had his sketching pad with him, and some of his finest landscapes came from those picnics. Someday I'll show you the paintings in the studio."

This was the opening Josie had been aching for. Every moment that she had she examined Mr. Van Dyk's paintings that hung on the walls of the house. But Miss Laura had told her that they were mostly early canvases and that the bulk of his work as yet unsold was locked in his studio. Josie was well aware of that locked door. She had stood before it wondering if she would ever get inside.

"Will you show them to me? I'd love to see them. . . ."

"Someday. Not today. Today's the day for a picnic. Besides I have to be in the right mood to go into that room," Miss Laura added, her face clouding over. "It's not easy for me."

Josie was down in the kitchen, cleaning up the breakfast dishes and making a list of what to get at the village store for the picnic, when Miss Laura called her from upstairs. "Josie, Josie. Come here, we have to go up to the attic."

Josie dropped what she was doing and went up to the bedroom. "What's up in the attic?"

"I can't find my big hat. I must have it. Come up with me to look for it."

The stairs to the attic were steep, and Josie walked nervously in back of Miss Laura fearing that she would fall. That attic was broiling hot, but Miss Laura was determined to go through the several trunks stored there.

"It's too hot here," Josie said. "You'll wear yourself out."

"I have to have my hat," Miss Laura insisted, pulling old clothes, packages of faded letters, dozens of pairs of shoes out of one trunk after another. But there was no big hat. Miss Laura was almost in tears. "It's got to be here. I put it here myself. I know I did."

Josie was afraid to remind her that she had thought it was in her bedroom closet. "We'd better go downstairs. You'll get sick if you say up here."

"You're talking to me as if I were a child," Miss Laura said indignantly. "You're mocking me."

"I'm not, honestly I'm not." But Josie was worried and frightened. Miss Laura looked very pale, and Josie herself was feeling the heat. Suddenly she wondered what in the world she was doing up in a broiling attic with this crazy old lady. "That hat is not here," she said firmly, "and we are going back downstairs."

"You are not to order me around in my own house," Miss Laura said sharply. "I am mistress of this house. I give the orders."

"That's what my grandfather says," Josie said unthinkingly.

"I'm sure he does," Miss Laura retorted. "I like young people, but not when they think they own the world. They don't. You think anyone who's old doesn't know anything, but you're wrong." She puttered about for another ten minutes or so and then finally annouced that she was ready to go downstairs. Much to Josie's relief, she allowed Josie to hold her hand going down the steep stairs.

Triumphantly, Josie found the hat in a guest-room closet. "Someone put it here to play a trick on me," Miss Laura complained. "They're always trying to trip me up."

Josie didn't know who "they" were, and she didn't ask.

Mrs. Thompson was in the kitchen when Josie got

back down here. She had walked over from her own house in the village. Now she announced that she was taking Miss Laura's car to the shopping center to do the marketing for the week.

"But you can't," Josie told her. "We're going on a picnic."

"She can go on a picnic another day. I have to market today. She won't know the difference. She's probably forgotten about it by now anyway."

"I don't think so," Josie said. "She has her heart set on it."

"One day is like any other to her. You don't know her the way I do. Like a child. Tell her the car broke down or something. I want to do some cooking and baking today, so I have to market."

Josie felt helpless. She didn't know what to do. Mrs. Thompson was a plump, brisk woman with a determined air, and Josie felt no match for her. She had worked for Miss Laura before, and she probably did know her better than Josie did. But it was with a sinking heart that Josie watched her take the car out of the garage. Josie could only hope that Miss Laura would forget about the picnic and get involved with something up in her room.

But in a few minutes Miss Laura's clear, high voice was calling, "Josie, Josie, come here, please."

Obediently and apprehensively, Josie trotted upstairs again. What now? she thought. Miss Laura had four long skirts draped over her bed, and she was studying them thoughtfully. "I can't decide which one to wear," she said. "What do you think?"

Josie was stumped. Should she tell the woman that the picnic was off, or should she play along with her and make up some excuse later? She wanted to put off telling her as long as possible, so she simply said, "They're all pretty." The whole situation was crazy. What difference did it make what Miss Laura wore to a picnic that was not going to take place? Josie felt as if she were in the Nutty House in the amusement park.

"Well, you press them all, and then I'll decide which one I want to wear." Miss Laura's serious face and voice made the whole situation more ludicrous than ever.

Josie's eyes kept turning to the clock as she ironed the skirts. It would soon be time for lunch, and then what would happen?

"Hurry up, Josie, it's time for us to go," Miss Laura called from upstairs. "Damn that Mrs. Thompson," Josie said to the air, pushing the iron too vigorously. She giggled nervously to herself as she thought about writing this story to Debbie. Imagine a woman in her eighties making such a fuss about a silly picnic.

Josie took the skirts upstairs and, still playing for time, told Miss Laura that she was going to take the car out of the garage. Maybe by some miracle Mrs. Thompson would get back. But she knew that was a hopeless thought since the shopping center was several miles away, and she also knew that when Mrs. Thompson went shopping in Miss Laura's car, she took care of a lot of errands for herself.

Laura walked out into the empty garage feeling like an idiot. What to do? Maybe if she stayed away long enough, pretending to have trouble getting the car started, Miss Laura would forget about the picnic. Her mind was like a sieve anyway. Josie stayed out in the garage as long as she dared and finally went back to the house and up to Miss Laura.

"I can't get the car started," she said.

"What's the matter with it? You probably flooded it. Paul used to do that."

"No, there's something wrong."

"Then call the garage. Tell them to send someone over immediately."

"It's lovely out in the garden. Why don't we have a picnic there?"

Miss Laura wrinkled her aristocratic nose. "No, I want to go for a ride and see someplace different. Go ahead, child, get busy. The day will be gone."

Josie couldn't stand it any longer, and besides why should she protect Mrs. Thompson? "Mrs. Thompson took the car," she blurted out, her heart quaking.

Miss Laura stared at her, and then her face crinkled up as if she were going to cry. "You were lying to me." Her face was so hurt that Josie felt terrible. But then Miss Laura drew herself up to her full height, her blue eyes blazing. "Everyone lies to me. I hate all of you. Just because I'm eighty-seven years old you think I don't know anything, you think I should be put away on the shelf. You looked sympathetic and kind, but you're all alike. You want to rob me, ignore me. You think old people should be shoved aside, stepped on. Let me tell you, if you're lucky you'll be old someday too. You'll get wrinkled, and your body will sag, and people will look at you with pity, wondering why you're hanging around, why you aren't dead. Well, I'm not dead. I'm very much alive. Go away. Leave me alone." She hurled the skirts to the floor and almost shoved Josie out of the room.

Josie went down to the kitchen. The sandwiches and fruit and wine, all neatly wrapped, were on the counter. She sank down on a chair, feeling shaken. Yes, she had been thinking all the things Miss Laura accused her of, except robbing. She didn't know what she meant by that. But old people were peculiar. Like her grandfather, Miss Laura got foolish notions she was stubborn about. She was demanding, forgetful, and repeated herself. Old people were boring and bossy. Josie didn't know what to think. Mrs. Thompson, who was older than she and knew Miss Laura better, had said don't pay any attention to her, yet she, Josie, was the one who had been yelled at.

Josie was still sitting despondently in the kitchen when Mrs. Thompson came back from marketing. While helping to carry in the groceries, Josie explained what had happened.

"Don't worry about it," Mrs. Thompson counseled her. "You should have given her her lunch and paid no attention. I let what she says go in one ear and out the next. I'll call her down for lunch now. Don't give her the sandwiches. That might remind her. Fix her an egg salad; she likes that. I've got to get to my baking."

Obediently Josie made an egg salad and, even though it was almost three o'clock, called Miss Laura and told her it was time for lunch. Quietly Miss Laura came downstairs. But she wasn't dressed. She wore a light robe over her nightgown, and Josie thought she looked very old and sad as she ate her lunch with a hopeless, almost vacant look in her usually bright eyes.

Josie was so depressed that she asked permission to go home for a couple of hours. Miss Laura nodded and said, "Go ahead. I'm tired today, and I'll stay in."

Once outside, Josie didn't feel like going home. The day was still bright and clear, and she thought that it would have been nice to have a picnic by a stream and dangle her feet in the cool water. She walked away from the village and took a path in the woods, but she couldn't shake off her depression. Her thoughts kept coming back to Miss Laura, and she wondered what the old woman was doing, sitting home in her room alone. After a while she sat down on a rock and stretched out her legs, her own, strong, tanned, smooth legs. Would they one day get veined and saggy like Miss Laura's and her round, firm arms have folds of skin and liver spots? Josie pointed her toes and stretched her arms above her head as far as they would go, feeling the strength and litheness of her young body against the hardness of the rock, and tried to dispel all her dismal thoughts. She was young and strong, and Miss Laura was seventy long years away from where she was. Maybe by the time she grew up people would never grow old. The scientists would discover a new miracle drug. Anyway she wasn't going to worry about it now. She had a job, she was living in an elegant house, and if Miss Laura hated being old that was her problem. There was nothing she, seventeen-year-old Josie, could do about it.

Four

It was a cool, wet morning, and Josie was standing out in the garden, her hair and clothes dripping, calling "Heloise, Heloise," as loud as she dared. She had hardly slept a wink all night worrying about the cat, which had disappeared the previous evening. So far Heloise's absence had not been noticed, and Josie was praying the cat would return before Miss Laura found out.

But Josie's hopes were soon dashed. Miss Laura was calling from the porch. "Josie, Josie, come here. What on earth are you doing out there in the rain? Come here at once!"

Josie tried to shake off some of her wetness as she stood in front of Miss Laura. "I felt like getting a little air," she said foolishly.

"Don't lie to me. Don't take me for a fool!" Miss Laura said irritably. "What were you doing?"

"I was looking for Heloise."

Miss Laura paled. "My Heloise, out in this weather? She'll get pneumonia and die. How did you ever leave her out, you careless girl. I won't have anyone in my house who doesn't take care of my cat. I suppose you don't put any value on a cat's

31

life, but every life is valuable, you understand? No, you don't, I can see by your face that you don't. Go away, get out of my sight, go away."

Up in her room Josie didn't know what she was supposed to do. She didn't know whether she was fired or not. Never in her life had anyone spoken to her like that, and if it had been anyone but Miss Laura she would have answered back. Her anger was boiling within her, and she started packing her clothes. Her father had been right; she couldn't last on this job! She had just succeeded in getting her suitcase down from the top of the closet when Miss Laura's shrill voice was calling her again.

"What is it, Miss Laura?" Josie called from the top of the stairs.

"What are you doing? Come down here."

"I thought you told me to go away."

"Maybe I did, but I need you now. Hurry up."

Downstairs Josie found Miss Laura fumbling with the key to the studio door, trying to open it. "This wretched key never works right," Miss Laura said. "You try it."

Josie opened the door easily. "I thought you wanted me to leave," she said.

Miss Laura looked at her wide-eyed. "I never said such a thing." Her clear blue eyes looked straight into Josie's. "I do not like anyone to be careless with my cat. But I daresay Heloise will turn up. She is very clever and can take care of herself. Just never let it happen again. Right now I have important business."

Josie wondered if she would ever get used to the vagaries of this woman's moods, her ups and downs, her irascibility, and her quick demands. And yet there was something grand about her as now she swept into her husband's studio that Josie could not help admiring. Though Josie had been dying to get into this room, she had also been afraid of tears and a big emotional scene from Miss Laura, but she appeared very much in control of herself.

The studio had obviously been an addition to the old house and reached up a story and a half, a huge room with a great span of white walls, hung with paintings, and a glass-domed roof that let in the light. Along two of the long walls, racks held what looked to Josie like several hundred paintings. There were no furnishings in the room except for a drawing table, an easel, a few chairs, and the paintings on the walls. The starkness of the studio was awesome, and yet Josie felt something extremely personal about it, as if she were stepping into its owner's personal life. Her eyes searched the paintings. There were a few landscapes and some abstractions, but the ones that interested her most were city and street scenes and people. Obviously Miss Laura must have been the model for many of the figures: a young woman in a rocker with two cats in her lap, a woman wearing a huge hat in a garden, a woman standing in front of a mirror brushing her hair. . . . Miss Laura with a lovely and younger face and figure looked back at her from many of the canvases. Josie could not tear her eyes away from one painting in particular, when Miss Laura must have been very young, maybe not much older than Josie was now. It showed a young woman sitting in a field of wild flowers with a bunch of daisies in her hand, with a wistful, hopeful, dreamy expression on her face amid the color and freshness of the spring flowers surrounding her. It was a beautiful painting, but it made Josie feel sad. Suddenly she wanted to put her arms around Miss

Laura, with her wrinkled throat and baggy arms, and say, "It must be terrible to grow old."

Miss Laura had been going through some of the paintings in the racks when she looked up and saw Josie's face. She followed Josie's eyes to the painting of herself as a young woman, and she smiled, not a sad smile. "That was a beautiful time," she said. She looked back at Josie. "Don't look so unhappy. That was a lovely time in my life, but it's over with. Don't be afraid of getting old, my dear. Every time in your life has its own beauty and its own sadness. That's the great thing about life; each period is unique, different from the one before. I have my fun now in my eighties."

She had a mischievous look on her face. "Some people think I'm dotty, and sometimes I am, but I know what I'm doing, don't worry." Then she drew herself up and looked conspiratorial. "They try to treat me like a child. They want to rob me, but they're not going to do it. Not any one of them, you'll see."

Josie didn't know what she was talking about, but she let it pass. "The paintings are beautiful," she said. "I wish I could paint like that."

"Do you want to be an artist?"

"More than anything in the world."

"Good, I can help you. But right now we have to get busy. A horrible little man is coming here this afternoon, an art dealer, who thinks he's going to swindle me out of Paul's paintings. He things he's going to buy them cheap because I'm a helpless old woman, and he hopes to make a fortune with them five or ten years from now. There's always a big revival of an artist's paintings five or ten years after he's dead. When I think of the years Paul slaved before he was recognized. . . ." Her voice trailed off, and she was gone again into the world of her past.

But Miss Laura soon recovered herself and gave Josie orders. "I want to turn over every one of these paintings and pick out a few to sell to him. I could use some money, and it will keep him happy. I'll sit here, and you pull out the canvases."

Miss Laura pulled up a chair and sat down, and Josie proceeded to remove the paintings from the rack one by one for Miss Laura to look at. Miss Laura kept up a running commentary. "Paul was in a bad mood when he painted that; he was never satisfied with it. We'd had a fight — oh, we fought, some terrible battles. Two people with temperament, what can you expect? But our fights never lasted long. Except once, when I left him for two weeks. I went off with another man just for spite, but I cried all the time for Paul. . . . Put that one aside. The little idiot can have it. Never that one. I'll never sell that. He painted that in Capri, and what a beautiful time we had there. We had been dreadfully poor, and finally Paul was going to have his first one-man show and he gave this painting to me. The gallery man was furious. He wanted it badly, but Paul wouldn't give in. . . ."

By the time they had gone through almost half the paintings, Josie was exhausted pulling the canvases in and out of the racks. But Miss Laura didn't seem to notice. She was reliving her life, each painting bringing back a memory, a series of events, as if each canvas were a page in a diary that she was reading. Josie's arms were aching, and yet she did not want to complain; she felt that she was witness to an important event, and she could sense the woman's feelings for the paintings. They were her life-line, her connection with the world she knew and the life she had lived. Even the few that she set aside to sell she had difficulty parting with, taking one out, putting it back, considering and reconsidering.

"My husband never really liked to sell a painting," Miss Laura said, "and now I feel the same way. It's like chopping out a piece of our life together. Each drawing and picture he made had its own place, its own background and story, and once it's gone we don't have it anymore."

Josie sat and watched Miss Laura primping in front of the mirror. She was ready to take a nap, but Miss Laura was wide awake, experimenting with her hair, fussing with it until she got it to her liking. She had had Josie put on and take off three different dresses before she had selected the one she wanted to wear. Josie had to keep herself from screaming. "You silly old fool," she wanted to yell, "who do you think's going to look at you? What difference does it make what you wear, how you look? You don't even like the man who's coming!" Twenty times a day she thought she couldn't go on with the job. She couldn't stand an old woman being so vain, so changeable in her moods, one minute going off into outer space and the next demanding to see the grocery bill.

Now they were getting ready for the art dealer to arrive, but Miss Laura acted as if royalty were coming. She was examining her face in a hand mirror. "I don't mind the fine wrinkles so much," she said, "but I hate my neck. It looks so old."

"You *are* old, you silly old thing," Josie wanted to say, but she held her tongue.

36

"Give me a scarf," Miss Laura ordered. "The small pink-chiffon one."

Josie looked through a drawer full of scarves before she found the right one, and then tied it around Miss Laura's throat as she directed. "Now we will go downstairs."

When Mr. Gallagher arrived, Miss Laura was all charm. Josie served them tea in the library and had difficulty keeping a straight face listening to Miss Laura tell him how pleased she was that he had come to buy some of her husband's paintings and how she had selected a few of his finest canvases to show him. She's an old devil, Josie thought, but she saw that Miss Laura was really enjoying herself. She was having a terrifically good time. Josie had never imagined that anyone that old could have any fun, could tell lies, could play a game the way Miss Laura was playing it. She had always thought that once you got that old, life had to be dreary and boring and depressing, just sitting around waiting to die.

"I wouldn't sell his paintings to just anyone," Miss Laura was saying. "Of course, you know that all the galleries are dying to get their hands on them, but I'm being very selective as to where they're going. . . ." Her face was as innocent as a child's, but her eyes were twinkling as she shot a glance at Josie.

After their tea, Miss Laura and the art dealer were in the studio for a long time. Josie waited outside, doing a few things around the house, wondering why she should care how many paintings Miss Laura sold. It was none of her business what the old thing did, and yet she was excited and anxious to know what was happening behind the closed door.

At last they came out, and she was asked to help carry four canvases out to Mr. Gallagher's station wagon while he sat down in the library to write out a check. When he finally left, Miss Laura was like a child, giggling and waving the check in the air. "The old fool," she said, speaking of a man some twenty or twenty-five years her junior, "he thinks he's got the cream of the cream. What he knows about art would fit inside a thimble. Now the next thing we have to do is to sit down and make a list of all my bills. Then we'll see what we can pay."

Josie had expected Miss Laura to be tired by now, but the woman was indomitable. She didn't even want to stop for supper, although Josie persuaded her at least to have some sandwiches while they did the accounts.

Josie had never seen so many bills in her life. She made lists and added columns up and down, but every time she needed to ask a question of Miss Laura, the older woman suddenly was half asleep, or she would wave her arm and say, "I can't be bothered with these things. Just add them up and see what they come to."

Josie grew more and more annoyed. When Miss Laura wanted to be wide awake she could be, and Josie had thought it silly to tackle the bills now anyway. Yet here she was stuck with this stupid job and not understanding half of it. Her empathy with Miss Laura flowed like the tide, rising and falling as the old woman's moods changed.

When Josie finally came up with a figure and told it to Miss Laura, she laughed. "It's two thousand dollars more than the check I got. Well, some of it will just have to wait."

Josie was shocked. "You mean you haven't the

money to pay these bills? Why didn't you sell more paintings?"

Miss Laura opened her drowsy eyes. "What for? They can wait for their money. I'm only selling what I have to, and then only a few things I don't care so much about. I'm not about to give away a fortune in my husband's work to pay some stupid bills."

"You're like my grandfather. He won't sell his land. I think he's stupid."

Miss Laura's eyes were suddenly sharp. "That's because you're young. You don't understand. His land is probably precious to him. All of you young people are alike. You're so self-righteous about your youth, and you want to take over. You want to turn everything into money, and you think old people have no feelings, that nothing matters anymore. What you don't understand, no one understands, is that people get old on the outside, but inside you still *feel* — even when your brain starts to go and you forget and you repeat and you get confused — you still have emotions, pride and jealousy and anger and hurt and love. Those things don't go; they become sharper if anything."

Josie was frightened by the agitation on Miss Laura's face. What if she had a heart attack or a stroke? But in a moment or two Miss Laura was dropping off again. Josie was moved by her words, and yet as she gathered up the sheaf of bills it seemed to her the irrationality of old age that made a woman run up a bunch of bills — some of them for the wildest extravagances in Josie's eyes — and then sit on a fortune and not pay them. She had to be crazy.

Five

Josie ran in and out of her own house often when she went on errands for Miss Laura, but an afternoon off was a special occasion. This afternoon, however, was almost gone. Miss Laura had thought of one thing after another for her to do before she left, and now that she was home she didn't know what to do with herself. Debbie was still in Maine, and she had lost contact with her other friends. Besides they were busy, and she felt out of sorts.

Her house looked dingier to her than ever after the elegance of Miss Laura's lamps and rugs and fine furniture. Looking at her grandfather lolling in his rocker, his shirt stained with drippings from his breakfast egg, she felt all her discontent; all the frustrations of her job, merge into her feelings about him. "Why don't you put on a clean shirt? You don't have to sit around looking a mess. Haven't you any pride?"

Her grandfather raised his eyes, still a clear, steady blue, and looked at her. "Yeah, I got pride, but I don't give a damn how I look. Some people got pride in some things, others in other things. I got pride in this house; I got pride in those fields out there. Who cares how I look?"

"I care. I have to look at you. What's so great about this house? It's a dump."

"Maybe it is to you. You never built a house and lived in it all your life. You never plowed your fields with your own horses and grew most everything you ate. You never walked over the same fields for fifty years every season of the year, in snow, ice, blazing sun, saw the trees turn every fall till it was so beautiful you damn near wanted to cry." He looked down at his shirt. "So what's a little egg on my shirt? That don't change nothing." He looked up at her again, and she saw the same expression in his eyes she had seen in Miss Laura's when she had been looking at her husband's paintings: defiance and pride, saying "don't anyone dare take this away from me."

"A clean shirt won't spoil anything either," Josie said in a kinder voice. "I'm going to get you one."

Her grandfather grinned. "Go ahead, girl, if it makes you happy."

Josie helped her grandfather into a clean shirt and combed his hair with a wet comb the way he liked it. "Straight back," he said. "No part."

He didn't say anything when she was finished, but she thought he sat up straighter in his chair. After a while he said, as if he were continuing a conversation, "Old people ain't that much different from young ones. Whatever they was, they're more so. I never did care about clothes, even when I was courting your grandmother. She used to scold me about buying new pants and things. Had to drag me to the store to buy a suit for our wedding. Seemed a waste of money to me. Druther have a new plow."

Josie was trying to decide if she wanted to ask him to tell her about his wedding when the telephone rang. It was Miss Laura. "You'd better come right home. We can't find the car keys. Mrs. Thompson has looked everywhere, and I want her to take me to the store."

"I put the keys on the kitchen counter. Mrs. Thompson knows where they are."

"She says she can't find them."

"Let me talk to her."

"She's busy. You come back here."

"I'll be back soon. In a little while. Mrs. Thompson will find the keys I'm sure."

Josie put the receiver back gently. But whatever gentle thoughts about aged people she had begun to have were rapidly disappearing. The old thing only wanted to get her back there, on her one afternoon off. "Can you imagine," she said indignantly, "calling me and telling me to come back on my time off?"

Her grandfather chuckled. "Means she likes you. Wants to have you around. Sometimes it gets lonesome."

"She has Mrs. Thompson there."

"Guess she likes you better. Doesn't want to lose contact. When you get old you can get awful scared of being left alone. You get bad thoughts. No one wants to die alone or be with someone who doesn't care."

"What makes her think I care?" Josie muttered.

Her grandfather had sharp ears. "You're a good girl, Josie. She knows you care. You get mad at old people 'cause you're fighting something in yourself. You're afraid of being swallowed up. But you won't be. You got your own life; you can walk away from it. Don't be afraid to give in. You got a good, gentle nature and a tough, hard one, and they can both do you some good if you give them their head."

It was almost suppertime when her parents came home. Her mother looked tired, and Josie helped her with their supper.

"Well, Josie, how you getting along with the old lady?" her father asked.

"All right, I guess." Her feelings about Miss Laura were so ambivalent that she didn't want to talk about them. A dozen times a day she thought she'd never last through the summer, but then Miss Laura would say or do something that was amusing or warm, and she'd change her mind. Also she didn't want to give her father the satisfaction of seeing her quit the job.

"Your cousin Mary's been trying to get hold of you," Mrs. Smyrski said. "About your fitting for your bridesmaid's dress."

Josie's face lit up. "Terrific. I've been so busy I almost forgot about the wedding."

"She's sending out the invitations and the banns were announced at church. It's just four weeks now. We decided to have the breakfast here for the wedding party. Then the dinner and reception will be at the firehouse."

"I'll have to get the day off," Josie said. "But why have the breakfast here?" Her voice implied that she didn't think much of that idea.

"It's the least I can do for my dead sister's daughter," her mother said.

"Josie doesn't think much of this house," her father said. "It ain't good enough for her."

"That's not it," Josie said, knowing full well that it was.

"She's living in a fancy place now," her grandfather said. "She's spoiled."

"I am not," Josie said indignantly, but her awareness of the contrast between her home and Miss Laura's made her feel guilty. Her grandfather had a way of hitting the mark with her. The thought of the wedding cheered her up, however, and she went to the phone to call her cousin. They arranged to meet to fit the bridesmaids' dresses on Josie's next day off.

After supper she said good-bye to her parents and to her grandfather. "What about them cabinets? They still there?" her grandfather asked.

"No, when the Van Dyks bought the house it was unfurnished."

"Too bad. They was beautiful cabinets. You tell that old lady about them, will you?"

"She won't care about them," Josie said, and then felt sorry because she could see she'd hurt her grandfather's feelings.

Walking back to Miss Laura's in the dusk, Josie thought about how hard it was not to hurt old people's feelings. Was it that they got more sensitive, or was it because they were on different wavelengths, treasuring their own memories that they didn't want anyone to spoil? Anyway, they sure were hard to deal with.

When Josie got back, Miss Laura had forgotten all about the car keys. She was excited, although not exactly happy, about some news she had to report. "They're coming up to spy on me, Paul's brother Henry and his wife. They pretend they come to see me, but I know better. They just want to get their

44

hands on Paul's paintings. I know what they're up to."

Mrs. Thompson rolled her eyes at Josie. "Now, now, dearie," she said addressing Miss Laura, "they're just looking out for your own good. They don't like to see you giving things away."

"They're mine to give away if I please," Miss Laura said indignantly. "Just a pair of busybodies, that's all," she muttered.

Later in the privacy of the kitchen, Mrs. Thompson confided in Josie. "They're good people, Mr. Henry and his wife. The old lady don't know nothing about handling her money. She don't know what goes on." Josie sat on a kitchen stool and watched Mrs. Thompson cut off several thick slices of ham and carefully wrap them up in silver foil. "My kids just love this kind of ham, and she won't miss it," Mrs. Thompson said without a blush.

"That's pretty expensive stuff," Josie commented.

Mrs. Thompson gave her a sharp look. "The way she throws money around it don't matter."

Josie was embarrassed by Mrs. Thompson. She didn't want to be in league with her against Miss Laura, but she didn't know what to do. She didn't want to seem a goody-goody prude nor make an enemy of Mrs. Thompson, but she was beginning to think that Miss Laura was a lot sharper than she was given credit for. She wondered if old people could get senile because they were treated that way, before the condition actually set in.

Miss Laura's relatives were not arriving until the next afternoon, and Miss Laura was very subdued in the morning. She wanted to sit in her husband's studio and asked Josie to pull out a few of his paintings. She sat and stared at them, and Josie wondered if she were really looking at them or if her thoughts were far away. Her face was sad. Suddenly she turned to Laura and said, "You said you were interested in being an artist. Show me what you have done."

Josie ran up to her room and brought down a folio of her drawings and watercolors. Miss Laura looked at them for a long time without saying a word. Again Josie wondered if she were actually seeing them or staring into space. She was ready to close up the folio and put it away when Miss Laura spoke to her in a quiet voice.

"They're not bad," she said. "I like the barn and the farmhouse. Your lines were freer, not so tight. That's what Paul always said of his students: the hardest thing was to get them to loosen up. If you look at that one and the drawing of the cats, you'll see the difference. I'll bet you did the cats much earlier."

Josie was surprised that Miss Laura remembered each picture so well. "You're right. I did the cats in class. I know what you mean. Thank you, thank you very much."

"Don't thank me. I've spent my life with a great artist, and I picked up a thing or two. Why not pass it on? Not that I think you're a genius, mind you, but you don't have to be a genius like Paul to enjoy painting."

"I thought someday I'd like to go to art school," Josie said.

"Mmm . . . maybe. Won't hurt you, but it takes more than talent. It takes a lot of drive and a lot of work. I'm not sure you're cut out to be an artist."

"I'm not sure either."

"Still, don't give it up. Painting for your own pleasure can make your life richer, more interesting."

"I do value your advice."

Miss Laura laughed gaily. "The old lady's not such a fool, is she?"

"I never thought you were a fool," Josie said guiltily.

"Of course you did. Everyone thinks so." Miss Laura sounded philosophic. "Sometimes I don't mind if they do," she added confidentially. "But sometimes," she said with a glare, "it makes me angry."

From the window, Josie watched the sleek Mercedes pull into the driveway and Celia and Henry Van Dyk got out. They were accompanied by a tall, long-faced boy with a droopy mustache and ink-black hair reaching to his shoulders. The boy was the image of his father, but the difference in their appearance was so striking that Josie had to laugh. The man was dressed impeccably, his dark business suit cut to perfection, and even in the midsummer heat he was wearing a buttoned shirt and tie. The boy was wearing a sports shirt, completely open, exposing a tanned chest. Cut-off jeans and leather sandals completed the effect. They looked like a study in opposites. Mrs. Van Dyk, in crisp, white linen, was a match for her husband.

Josie didn't want to intrude on the family greetings, but Miss Laura called her almost as soon as her guests were in the house and made the introductions. Then she announced in a loud voice, "Michael can have the small guest room on the second floor, and Henry and Celia may use the attic room on the third floor. I am now going to have a nap, and I do not wish to be disturbed. One more thing! No one is to go into Paul's studio."

Josie happened to be looking at Mrs. Van Dyk while Miss Laura was speaking, and she was startled by the frightened look on the woman's face. "Henry, I told you we should not have come. We've never been welcome in this house, and you know it. Let's go, please."

"Now Celia," her husband said patiently, as if this were old ground they'd been over before, "I owe it to Paul to see how Laura is getting along. We can't just leave her here with servants. It's not right. Everything will be all right, just take it easy. Remember Laura is getting on, and you mustn't get upset by everything she says. She doesn't mean it."

"That's what you think," Miss Laura said tartly. "It so happens that I have a very good memory. And I remember that you weren't so anxious to visit Paul when we were living in a horrible place on Fourteenth Street, and Paul was struggling. But I don't care where you sleep, as long as it's not Paul's room." She waved her arm airily.

"Whatever you want," Celia said apologetically. "I never did understand those two brothers. In my family we're not like that. . . ."

"I feel sorry for you, Celia." Miss Laura was suddenly being the grand lady again. "You have never understood that Henry has never forgiven Paul for being a successful artist. Did you never notice that there is not a painting of Paul's in your husband's house? When Paul's paintings were going for peanuts and Henry could have bought some to help, could have shown them to his rich friends, he never did. Paul didn't care, but I did. Paul always de-

fended Henry, God knows why. That was Paul; he
trusted everyone. Now the laugh's on Henry because
the paintings are worth thousands, and he doesn't
own one. He's never gotten over.that. It still makes
him mad." Miss Laura chuckled, and then her face
became serious. "Henry holds grudges for a long
time. Not like Paul. Henry was his little brother.
That was enough for Paul to forgive him anything."
She turned to Josie. "Come, help me up the stairs.
I'm tired."

Josie took Miss Laura's arm and up the stairs
they went with Heloise trotting behind them. Miss
Laura had a tired but thoughtful look on her face.
"It's Michael I worry about now," she said. "Henry
doesn't know what to make of him. He doesn't know
whether Michael's going to turn out to be someone
great like Paul, or nothing. I don't know either, but
then at nineteen no one has to know. When I was a
girl, the boys took their time. They traveled around
and played before they settled down. Now it's push,
push to get ahead. Michael's got a little money Paul
left him. He ought to go abroad. Would do him
good. I only hope he's not weak and scared like his
mother."

"I don't think he is," Josie said. "Of course, I
don't know him. . . ." Her voice trailed off.

"I hope you're right. Young people today know
how to break loose. Paul did, but Henry never could.
That's his trouble." Josie left Miss Laura resting
with her cat curled up at her feet.

When Josie came back downstairs, the Van Dyks'
suitcases were still in the hall, and Henry and Celia
were in the garden. Michael was sitting at the
kitchen table drinking a soda. He greeted Josie with

49

a grin. "I guess you got quite a load of my family. Not a good introduction."

"I wasn't paying attention," Josie lied.

Michael hooted. "Not paying attention to my father is something I've been trying to manage for many years. But how do you make out with my aunt?"

"We get along all right."

"She's mad as a hatter, but she likes me I think. I hope she lets me stay."

"Has she asked you to?"

"No, but I'm going to ask her. I'm her only nephew, and I'm supposed to be special. My dad was fifty when he got married, so I came as rather a surprise to the family. I think my parents are still surprised."

There was something frank and open about Michael that appealed to Josie, and yet she wondered what his motives were. Why did he want to stay? Was he sincere? It was not her business to question him. Damn it, she thought, I just work for Miss Laura. I'm not her keeper. But she did find herself resenting anyone she saw taking advantage of her boss.

"Miss Laura is not mad," Josie said. "She knows exactly what she's doing. Sometimes she gets confused or forgetful, but she's not crazy."

Michael looked at her in surprise. "Hey, she's got you hooked. Has she given you any paintings yet?"

"Certainly not." Josie glared at him. "I wouldn't accept one anyway."

"Why not, if she gives you a present? She will if she likes you. She gave a drawing worth hundreds to a gardener last spring. My parents went wild, wanted to put her away."

"Well, they're hers to do what she wants with them. No one has a right to stop her."

"Don't get mad at me. I'm on your side. I only hope I'm the one she gives them to."

Josie couldn't figure him out. At least he was honest about his feelings, but if he was only here to see what he could get out of Miss Laura, he must be pretty obnoxious. Again she had to tell herself it was none of her business what Michael or any of the Van Dyks did. Yet she was curious about Michael and couldn't help asking, "Are you on vacation from your job?"

Michael shook his head. "I haven't got a job. I'm a college drop-out. One year was enough for me. The trouble with me is I don't know what I want to do, much to my father's disgust. Do you?"

Josie was startled by his direct question. "Not really. I've thought about art school, but I'm probably not good enough."

Michael's warm grin changed his face. "You sound like me. I never think I'm good enough. I wish I were like my Uncle Paul; he had such confidence in himself."

"Your aunt believes in herself too."

"Let's hope some of it rubs off on us," Michael said.

Josie smiled in agreement.

Later, when Miss Laura came downstairs, Josie noticed that she was walking with quite a stoop to her shoulders. At first she thought the old woman was putting on an act, but her face did look tired.

"What are these things doing in the hall?" Miss Laura demanded, poking at one of the suitcases with her foot.

"They're ours," Henry said brightly. "We'll take them up soon."

"What are you doing here?" Miss Laura asked.

"We came before your nap. Don't you remember?"

She paid no attention to him and looked past him at his wife. "Who's she? What is she doing here?"

Celia looked frightened. "She's my wife," Henry said gently. "You know Celia."

"She's too young. Don't marry anyone that young, Henry. Only make a fool of yourself."

"We've been married twenty years, my dear. I guess you forget."

"Don't count on it, Henry. My memory's as good as yours."

At the dinner table Josie was worried. She had never seen Miss Laura look so frail and old and act so agitated. She kept dropping her food from her fork and picking it up with her fingers. She heedlessly broke into conversation between the Van Dyks with irrelevant remarks. They were talking about the garden when suddenly she said to Josie, "Where are my red shoes? I can't find them. I wish you wouldn't hide things on me."

"I don't hide anything," Josie said.

"Don't contradict me. I'm not a liar."

"Of course not." Josie saw the elder Van Dyks exchange meaningful glances, and so she added protectively, "Perhaps I did put them in the back of the closet."

Michael gave her an amused look but said nothing.

The meal was agonizing. Josie felt as if Miss Laura was going rapidly downhill before her eyes. When dinner was finally over and Josie was helping Miss Laura upstairs to her room, she heard Celia's little voice. "You're right, Henry. She has to be put away. She cannot go on in this house any longer. God knows what is going on. Oh dear. . . ."

"I'll take care of it, don't worry," Henry said in his officious voice, a voice that Josie decided could easily get on your nerves.

After Josie helped Miss Laura get undressed and into bed, the old woman, usually so proud and defiant, abruptly burst into tears. She clung to Josie sobbing. "Henry's come to destroy me. I'm frightened. I've never been afraid of him before, but I'm frightened now. Help me, please help me. Don't let him rob me, don't let him put me away. I'm old, but this is my home. I want to die here. I'm not afraid of dying, but I'm afraid of him."

Josie held Miss Laura in her arms and tried to soothe her. She was frightened by her outburst and her trembling and held her close. "It's all right. No one will hurt you. I won't let them. I promise I won't."

She stayed with Miss Laura until she fell asleep. Before Josie left the room she picked up Heloise and settled her on the bed in the curve of Miss Laura's frail body. She was sure she heard Miss Laura sigh with pleasure. Then Josie turned out the light and tiptoed out of the room.

Six

Lying awake that night, Josie thought about the promise she had made. It had been an emotional commitment, and now she was wondering whether she really meant it. She did not want to become involved in Miss Laura's life or affairs — a summer job was enough — but the old woman had been sad and frightened, and Josie had spoken spontaneously. Miss Laura had said that she was not afraid of dying, but how could an old person not be afraid to die? Perhaps, Josie thought, when you do get old and you can't run and jump and do all the things you did when you were young, dying doesn't hold the same terror. Josie didn't want to die. Yet she didn't want to grow old and be like Miss Laura. But unless she did die, she would grow old. She shuddered under the covers. She was thinking seriously for the first time about life and death, and it was frightening.

Josie thought about her grandfather and felt a stirring of pride. He never talked about dying, but surely he must think about it. He seemed so connected with life, as if he was going to live forever, and spoke only casually about what would happen after he was gone. The *now* was what mattered to him, and she thought about the way she had badgered him about his fields. From her point of view it wasn't as if he *needed* the land, and yet maybe there was more than one kind of need: the way Miss Laura needed control of her husband's paintings and needed to be mistress in her home and of her life. Josie suddenly remembered the way she had cried and cried when her mother had thrown out a huge, dirty, old stuffed panda she had treasured for years, and her mother kept telling her that she didn't need it anymore. Josie had yelled, "I do need it, I do need it." She had been furious that her mother didn't understand — and she herself hadn't realized at the time — that with the panda part of her childhood had been thrown away. Miss Laura, like Josie's grandfather, was holding on to her life, wanting to keep her treasures, her hats and shoes and dresses, and wanting to be involved in everything that happened around her, in her house, in her own affairs.

Josie fell asleep with her thoughts going around in circles, worn out with the contradictions of her own feelings. She wished she had never become involved in taking care of an old lady, and yet she felt that she was on the brink of learning something about life that she might never have known otherwise.

The next morning there was a definite strain at the breakfast table. Celia Van Dyk looked white and perpetually frightened, Henry preoccupied, and Miss Laura wary. Only Michael seemed undisturbed. "How would you like a guest for a while, Aunt Laura?" he asked.

"Who?"

"Me, your ever-loving nephew. I thought I'd stay for a while if you'd like it."

"I don't mind."

"You're not exactly enthusiastic."

Miss Laura managed a smile. "We'll see how you behave, and if you make yourself useful."

"That would be a new twist," Michael's father said.

Michael flushed. "I'm turning into a good cook. I'll make you some crepes tonight, if you want. That's one thing I'm pretty good at."

"He really is," Celia said eagerly, avoiding her husband's eyes, which showed that he did not think much of his son as a cook.

Miss Laura's face lit up. "You inherit that from your Uncle Paul. Do you know that he was a gourmet cook? He didn't cook often, but when he did he was fabulous. *Blanquette de veau* was his specialty. It's really only a veal stew with onions and mushrooms, but such a lovely, delicate dish. He always liked the French veal better than the American — for some reason, American veal produces more scum, and that always annoyed Paul. Will you make it for me, Michael?"

"If you give me Uncle Paul's recipe, I'll try."

"Paul never used a recipe. He cooked by instinct. Paul was an artist in everything he did. But you'll find some good French cookbooks in the library, and there's certain to be a recipe for veal blanquette. We'll have it with artichoke hearts and a fine wine — We'll have a party, just us, you and Josie and me, and stuff ourselves. What fun!"

Josie giggled. "What's so funny?" Michael asked.

"I can't imagine you as a cook."

"You'd be surprised."

"Aunt Laura may not be staying here very long." Michael's mother spoke to her son in a foolish whisper she seemed to believe Miss Laura could not hear.

"And where do you think I'm going?" Miss Laura shot right back.

Henry gave his wife an annoyed look. "We'll talk about it later," he said.

"We'll talk about nothing except perhaps your departure. Do you wish to leave before lunch or after?"

"Oh, we'll leave right after breakfast," Celia said hurriedly.

"We will see," Henry said flatly. "You don't have to worry about our lunch, Laura. Mrs. Thompson will take care of it." His eyes were throwing daggers at his wife.

Josie had been listening to the conversation with embarrassment. It was easy to see that Miss Laura and her brother-in-law were old enemies. Still, Josie suspected that Miss Laura got a kick out of battling with him, except when she broke down as she had the night before. But Josie felt sorry for poor Celia. She seemed so afraid of her husband, probably even afraid of her son, or for him. It was hard to tell which. Celia could sure use some woman's lib, Josie thought, the way she cowered before Henry Van Dyk. Josie felt sorry for her, and at times, when she caught her looking at Miss Laura, she thought she admired the old lady and wished she had her guts. Michael was the one Josie couldn't figure out. It was pretty apparent that he did not get along with his father, and she couldn't blame him. But it was hard to tell if he sympathized with his mother or was as weak as she was.

One thing Josie was sure of: she did not want to be in the middle of a family quarrel. Stay out of it, she admonished herself, but she wondered if that would turn out to be possible.

It was sometime in midmorning that Josie heard a lot of shouting from the studio and her name called. She ran downstairs to see what the commotion was about.

Miss Laura and Mr. and Mrs. Van Dyk were in the studio, and Miss Laura's face was white with anger. Her head was bobbing with a frightening trembling motion.

"Josie, did you give these people the key to my husband's studio?"

Josie shook her head vehemently. "No, I did not. I haven't seen the key."

"I told you she didn't give it to us," Henry said.

"Then you stole it. You stole the key to come spying in here. This room is sacred. Do you understand that? This room is sacred to my beloved husband's memory, and only I decide who can enter it."

"Now, Laura, don't get yourself so excited. I have to see the paintings. You are behaving very foolishly. I only want to look at them."

"*Now* you're interested in Paul's paintings, now that he's dead, now that they're worth thousands. You want to get your hands on them, Henry. I know what you're up to. Josie, get their bags and show them to the door."

Josie looked at the Van Dyks helplessly. "Perhaps you had better go. She feels so strongly about this room. She treasures it."

Celia was fanning herself with a magazine and looked as if she might faint. "Henry, let's go, please. I told you we never should have come. It was a mistake."

"Everybody please calm down." Henry spoke like a top sergeant. "Laura, you have been putting off this inventory and putting it off, and in the meantime you've given drawings away and God knows what else. No one is trying to rob you. Face up to the facts. You're an old woman and a candidate for people to take advantage of — "

"Like you," Miss Laura cut in sharply. "I don't need you to protect me."

"Paul thought differently." Henry's voice was sharp now, too. "You saw the letter he left. I believe you have a copy of it, although you treat it like a joke. He asked me as his brother and a businessman to see that the paintings get disposed of to their best advantage. It's only for your good."

"I know what's for my good. I'm not senile yet. I don't know what possessed Paul to write such a letter, and it has no legal standing anyway. I'm sure you pushed him into doing it. But Paul's dead and I'm alive, and I'm not going to have you interfering in my affairs." She stared at her brother-in-law defiantly, but her voice trembled.

"I'm afraid you can't stop me. I intend to carry out the responsibility Paul entrusted me with. I will carry out his wishes."

Miss Laura's face crumpled. "Yes, I am an old woman and you are stronger than I am. But you're a stupid, insensitive man, Henry. You wear your responsibility like some rigid coat of armor that cannot bend with an old woman's feelings. My poor, dear Paul, he didn't know, he'll never know. . . ."

"Henry, let's go now," Celia pleaded. "The inventory's waited this long . . . maybe when Laura's feeling better, or when she isn't here it will be easier. . . ."

Miss Laura pulled herself up. "You are not going to put me out of my house. I don't care about your silly inventory. Come on, out you go." She actually gave Henry a push, which he tried to laugh off, but his face was flaming.

Miss Laura walked out of the room, leaning on Josie's arm. Josie wanted to put her arms around the old woman, but her instinct told her no. Miss Laura's pride, or what she had left of it, was the most precious thing she had. When they got to Miss Laura's room Josie had to keep back her tears when she saw Miss Laura's sad, crushed face. "Poor, dear Paul," Miss Laura murmured, "he loved to think of me as beautiful and gay and frivolous, and I was, but I don't need Henry now. Henry was a money-maker from the beginning, but he's still stupid. Paul refused to see that side of him. . . ."

Why, oh why, Josie wondered, did people like Henry treat old people as if they didn't count? She herself was guilty of doing the same thing to her grandfather, and she didn't think she was a bad person. The question troubled Josie deeply, and she didn't know the answers.

A little while later Josie was relieved to see Henry bring their suitcases downstairs. Apparently he had decided that this was not the best day to take his inventory. He took Josie aside before they left. "You're really too young for this job . . . typical of my sister-in-law to hire a kid. But here is my phone number, my office and my home." He handed her a card. "If she does anything with any of the paintings or drawings, I want you to call me immediately. She's sitting on a fortune in there, and the poor woman doesn't know what she's doing. And I wouldn't count on this job for too long, if I were you. We expect to take her to a place where she can be properly taken care of."

"She's well taken care of here, sir," Josie said.

"I'm sure you do your best," he said coolly, "but we think she needs professional care. She's very old and quite senile."

"She's pretty sharp, sir," Josie said.

Henry Van Dyk didn't bother to answer. "Come, Celia," he called to his wife. "Let's go."

Mrs. Van Dyk kissed Michael good-bye for the fourth time and finally followed her husband out the door.

Michael heaved a big sigh of relief when their car pulled out of the driveway. Josie couldn't help giving him a questioning look. After all, they were his parents. Michael grinned. "Yeah, I know they're my parents, and I'm a lousy son to want to be rid of them. But you don't know the half of it."

"I guess I don't," Josie said. She wasn't sure that she wanted to hear any of it. She did not want to get mixed up in the family affairs of the Van Dyks. Once again she reminded herself that her job was to take care of Miss Laura, and that was all, yet the Van Dyks and their cross relationships seemed to be enveloping her.

"I'll fill you in, if you want." Whether she wanted or not, he settled himself on the stairs and went on. "You heard my Aunt Laura. I think my father really hated his brother. Maybe *hate* is the wrong word, but he couldn't understand him so he had no use for him. Artists to him were queer — I don't mean fags, just oddballs, misfits — and when Uncle Paul became successful it was too much for my dad.

He's been furious with his own stupidity so he's belligerent, hostile. And now I'm the butt of it. He doesn't understand me because I like to cook, I collect things, I don't like nine-to-five jobs. According to my father, I'm not manly, not the gung-ho type. I'm the wrong kid for him, and he's being stupid and hostile all over again. And my mother. . . ." Michael shrugged. "I guess I feel sorry for her. She's weak, and she's scared of my father, and she's not sure herself whether I'm a bum or not. Maybe I don't know either, but at least I'm trying to find out. My father can't stand Aunt Laura, which is enough to put me on her side. So I came up here to do some thinking, and right now anything's better than living at home. So here I am."

Josie didn't know what to say to this confidential outburst. But she felt sympathy for Michael because she, too, had come to Miss Laura's to get away from home. She said as much to Michael. "It's funny that we both came here for almost the same reason. Miss Laura's seems to be some kind of a haven for unhappy kids."

"Maybe so," Michael said. "When you're around someone old like my aunt, it gives you a lot to think about. It's kind of scary, you know, that someday you can get that way, but it makes you want to give some meaning to what you do with those years in between."

"That's what Miss Laura thinks, too. She has an idea that you ought to go to Europe."

"I know, she's told me that. That's what she says young men did in her day. She forgets they were only the rich ones. I wouldn't mind going to Europe, but I think I'd rather know what I'm coming back to."

"Isn't there anything you really want to do?" Josie asked.

"I do like to cook. I was thinking maybe of going to a cooking school, a good restaurant school."

"Why don't you do it, go to a school?" Josie felt sympathy for him in his uncertainty, caught as he was between his mother's weakness and his father's shadow.

"Maybe I will. But what about you? You're not going to take care of old ladies all your life, are you? I suppose you want to get married. Most girls do."

"They marry men, you know," Josie said indignantly. "It takes two. I may get married someday. In the meantime, I guess I'm in the same boat you are, trying to figure out what I want to do."

Michael met her eyes and grinned. "I guess only two kooks like us would be spending the summer here with my batty aunt."

"She may be much less batty than we are," Josie said, only half-jokingly.

When Miss Laura came downstairs after her nap, she was bursting with energy. "Michael, I'm going to put you to work. The first thing is to clean up the cellar. Get rid of all the rusty old tools and put the rest in order. Last time I was down there it was a mess. I like to see everything hung up on nails. Get rid of all the old cartons and junk lying around."

"When were you last down in the cellar, Aunt Laura?"

Miss Laura closed her eyes. "Oh, about ten years ago I'd say."

"Then don't you think it could stay that way for another few days? It's hot today."

"No. I've been thinking about it, and I want it

63

done now. Work is good for you. Come on, get busy."

Michael made a grimace. "You are impossible," he muttered, as he got up lazily. He disappeared down the cellar steps but was back upstairs in a very short while. "There are rats down there. I'm not going near the place."

"Rats! We've got to get rid of them. I'll get the gun."

Josie was horrified. "You're not going to use a gun, Miss Laura?"

"No, but Michael will."

"Not me. No, thank you. I'm not going down to shoot rats."

"Then I will." Miss Laura left the room and came back carrying a light shotgun. "Come on, down we go."

"We can't let her." Josie turned to Michael. "You've got to stop her."

But Miss Laura was already at the head of the cellar steps. "My God," Josie cried, running after her. "She'll fall down the stairs and kill herself."

There was no stopping Miss Laura, and Josie and Michael, one on each side of her, accompanied her down the cellar stairs. Miss Laura stood, with gun poised, but no rats appeared. "There are no rats down here," she said. "Maybe you heard some mice."

"I saw a rat," Michael insisted.

"You're not telling me the truth, Michael. Thought you'd fool me. You go ahead and clean up down here. Now that I'm down here I can tell you what to do." She sat herself down on a wooden crate and gave him orders. His gloomy face made Josie laugh.

"You can't fool Miss Laura for long," Josie remarked. Michael glared at her. "I did see a rat," he insisted, but Josie was convinced he had made the story up so as to get out of the cleaning job.

Miss Laura laughed with glee. "Thought you had me fooled. Rats my eye."

Josie and Miss Laura left him to his cleaning and went upstairs.

When he finally joined them in the library, he was flushed with the heat. "Any place to swim around here?"

"There's a pool down the stream where we can go," Miss Laura said.

"I thought you might want to take a nap, and Josie and I could go for a swim," Michael told her.

"I don't want to nap. I'll go with you."

Michael gave Josie a pleading glance. "It's a rough walk down the stream. I think you ought to rest."

"Don't you tell me what to do, young man. I may not go in the water, but I'm not staying home. I'm going to get my sneakers."

Alone with Michael for a few minutes Josie said, "She likes to be involved with everything. She doesn't want to be left out."

"For God's sake, she doesn't have to tag along with us all the time, does she? She's old; we're young."

"I'm here on a job," Josie told him. "Besides, she likes to be with young people."

Michael looked at her curiously. "I thought you were here for the same reason I am, because you wanted to leave home."

"That was part of it. But I still have a job," Josie said with asperity. "What's that platter?" She just noticed a large, blue-and-white porcelain platter Michael had put on a bookcase and now picked up to examine.

"I found it down in the cellar. I know a little about these things. It's old and worth money. I want it for my collection, or maybe I'll sell it to an antique dealer. Bet I could get a couple of hundred bucks for it."

"But it's not yours. It's Miss Laura's."

"She didn't even know it was there. She won't notice. And you won't tell her, will you?"

"You can't sell it. Not without her permission."

"What does she need it for? She's old; she doesn't need it. Probably it was down there for years. Don't you go be a tattletale."

Josie looked at the long, boney face and thought, This is all I need here, to have this kook around. "I'm not a tattletale, but I think it's disgusting. What if she asks for it?"

Michael shrugged. "Don't be silly. She never will."

Josie found herself inordinately annoyed with him. Then it occurred to her that she might have done the same thing to her grandfather if she had been able to get away with it, and she realized that a large part of her annoyance was guilt.

When Miss Laura came downstairs she had on her sneakers, and with them a long, full skirt, square-necked blouse, and her beloved straw hat. The carried a pair of white gloves.

"Where do you think you're going?" Michael asked.

"Out. We're going out, aren't we? My mother used to say you never know but what you may meet your future husband. Perhaps I'll meet Paul."

"Paul is dead. Aunt Laura, perhaps you'd better rest."

"I know Paul is dead. Who should know better than I? But I may meet him just the same. Who knows?"

Michael heaved a long sigh and whispered to Josie behind Miss Laura's back, "She *is* balmy. Maybe my parents are right."

"Sh-sh," Josie said. "She goes off sometimes, so what? I bet you do too sometimes."

"Stop whispering, you two. I hate whispers. Let's go."

The path to the stream was overgrown, and the going was rough. The two young people went slowly to accommodate Miss Laura, who made quite a sight walking daintily through the brush in her sneakers, picking up her long skirt and peering at them from under her wide-brimmed hat.

When they reached the natural pool nestled under tall hemlocks, Miss Laura was ecstatic. "If ever Paul comes back," she said, "this is where I'll find him. I think he loved this spot better than any place in the world. We traveled all over, but he always wanted to come home to this. Do you believe in life after death?" she asked, looking at Josie wistfully.

Josie hesitated. It would have been nice to humor the old woman whose eyes were so intent on hers, but if she did that, she would be falling into the very trap she was beginning to resent. No, she was going to treat her as a person who could understand. "To be honest, I do not," Josie said. "I think that if there were a life after death, we'd know about it by now. I can't go along with all that religious stuff. No, I believe that when life is finished, it's finished. Whatever is left returns to the earth. But your husband lives in his paintings," she added gently.

Miss Laura nodded. "I know. I have fantasies about an afterlife, but I'm afraid they are fantasies. But sometimes a fantasy can be very comforting."

"Come on, let's go swimming," Michael said impatiently.

"All right, all right." Josie followed him into the cool water. "You see, she can be rational when you don't get her all upset by treating her like an idiot," she said to Michael, as they sat on a rock with their feet dangling in the water.

"Wouldn't you like to live this way? I mean without Aunt Laura, just go swimming, eat, be lazy, do what you feel like doing?" Michael asked.

"It might get boring," Josie said.

"Are you one of those people who has to be busy, has to have a purpose all the time?"

Josie threw a pebble into the water and watched it make ripples. "They're two different things. Just being busy is one thing, and having a purpose is another."

"That's very wise," Michael commented.

Josie laughed. "You sound surprised. I suppose you think I'm a dumb country girl."

Michael flushed. "I keep wondering why you took this job."

"I took it because I needed money. Plain and simple. Now it's a lot more than money, though."

"Is it just Aunt Laura who's interesting you here?" Michael gave her a sly look.

It was Josie's turn to flush, but she met his eyes candidly. "If you're asking me am I glad you're here, the answer is most of the time." Then she laughed. "And that's all you're going to get out of me." But she wondered what his answer would be if she asked him the same question.

Miss Laura was very cheerful when they joined her again. She started recalling some of the picnics and moonlit swims she and her husband used to have by the pool. One story led to another, and Miss Laura charmed them as she talked. "One time, Paul and I were skinny dipping when we heard a shot. Forgetting he was naked, Paul went running out into the woods calling, 'Who's there, who's there?' A couple of young boys were illegally hunting raccoons at night, but when they saw this crazy naked man running toward them, they were scared silly and ran for their lives. Guess they thought he was a ghost. Paul and I laughed ourselves sick. Served them right for wanting to kill those adorable raccoons."

That evening Miss Laura decided that Michael should make a cheese soufflé for supper. "But I've never made a soufflé," he protested.

"Then it's high time you learned. Come, I will teach you." Miss Laura marched into the kitchen and sat down on a high kitchen stool and gave directions to Michael. "Josie, you set the table," she ordered. "We have to eat the minute the soufflé is ready. Otherwise, it will collapse."

"I'll collapse first," Michael said, running back and forth across the large kitchen on Miss Laura's orders. His forehead was dripping with perspiration, but it was obvious that he was having a good time. "My parents don't appreciate my cooking."

"Your father is a meat-and-potato man, and your mother knows absolutely nothing about good food.

I'm glad you are carrying on Paul's tradition of fine eating."

When the table was set, Josie sat down in the kitchen, too. She felt a wave of pleasure at being there. The kitchen was cosy, the food smelled delicious, and it was easy to forget that Miss Laura was a very old woman and could be an outrageously demanding one.

While they were eating, Miss Laura's sharp eyes spied the blue-and-white platter that Michael had carelessly left on the sideboard. "Where did that come from?" she demanded.

"Damn," Michael muttered. "It's an old thing I found down in the cellar," he told her.

"You're darn right it's an old thing. Worth a few hundred dollars."

"You're cuckoo. It's a piece of junk. I was going to throw it out."

"Is that way you left it on the sideboard?" she asked shrewdly. "Didn't you tell me not so long ago you knew something about old chinaware?"

"A little bit."

"Michael, you're not a very good liar. I don't know whether that's good or bad. Lying is a fine art." She gave him her mischievous smile. "I had a beautiful day today, so I'll make you a present of that platter. If you want to junk it, you can. If not, you may get some money for it."

"That's fantastic, Aunt Laura! Terrific!" He kissed her cheek with a sheepish smile.

"That's twice in one day she got onto you," Josie said with a touch of malice.

"Don't rub it in."

After dinner, before going up to her room, Miss Laura said, "Michael, help Josie clean up and do the dishes. I'm not going to let you just loaf around here. And I like everything washed up at night; no dirty dishes left until morning."

"Yes, Aunt Laura," Michael said docilely.

When Josie came downstairs after helping Miss Laura get ready for bed, Michael hadn't moved a dish. "I thought you were going to start cleaning up."

"What's the hurry?"

"She likes to have everything cleaned and put away."

"She's upstairs. She won't know the difference."

"I suppose not." Josie sat down opposite Michael. "It was a nice afternoon. She really enjoyed it."

"Didn't you?"

Josie nodded. "Yes, I did. She once said to me that you could have fun in your eighties. I couldn't believe her. But she did have fun today, talking about her life. I always get annoyed when my grandfather talks about the past, but he enjoys it too."

"I hope I die young," Michael said. "I don't want to get old."

"That's a terrible thing to say. Maybe being old isn't so awful. I mean if people are nice to you."

"They're only nice to you if you're rich. And then they can't wait for you to die."

"That's not true," Josie said indignantly. "My parents are very good to my grandfather, and he's not that rich. I'm the one who hasn't been," she added thoughtfully. "I've hoped he would die. Isn't that awful?"

Michael shrugged. "It's natural, I guess."

Josie didn't answer. She was thinking about what Michael had said about waiting for someone to die because he was rich. She had wanted her grandfather to die so that they could sell the land, but that was only part of it. She also thought he had nothing to live for, just sitting and looking at his fields, dreaming about the past, as if that were enough to keep him alive. Did he really enjoy his life? she wondered.

When she turned to Michael, she said, "I think being rich is probably very important to you."

"What makes you say that?"

"You seem to want a lot of things without working."

"I wouldn't object. But I don't want to work just to make money. I want to enjoy what I do. Don't you?"

"Of course, who doesn't? But I think I'm changing my mind about money."

"How?"

"I used to think about it so much. It's a long and complicated story and has to do with my grandfather." She didn't want to tell him about how she had felt about the old man's acres.

"I think when people get old they don't care so much about money. They don't need it, except if they're really poor."

Josie studied his face for a moment. "You'd like your aunt to give you some money now, wouldn't you?"

He looked startled by her question. "That's a hell of a thing to say. You think I came up here to get something out of her, don't you?"

"I'm not sure."

"Well, maybe I did have some crazy notion, but I haven't now. Listen, Josie, I'm not much on expressing feelings, but she's a pretty important person to me, you understand?"

"Yes, I think I do. I'm sorry if I said the wrong thing."

"It's okay. So long as we understand each other, okay?"

"Okay." She turned away, wondering what other people were important to this strange boy. She wouldn't have asked him, and she didn't have a chance anyway. Michael changed the conversation to food, one of his favorite topics. It was also, Josie realized, a safe one because he knew a lot about cooking and the subject was free of emotional content.

They sat and talked awhile until Josie got up and said, "Come on, let's clean up."

Michael yawned. "I'm too sleepy now. We can stack the dishes in the sink and do them in the morning. She'll never know."

"Sometimes she comes down early for a cup of tea before I bring up her breakfast tray. I leave water in the kettle and a tea bag out for her, just in case."

"Then she'll see some dirty dishes. Won't hurt her. I'm going to bed."

Josie hesitated. "All right, I'll leave them."

Upstairs in her room, Josie couldn't fall asleep. There were too many thoughts going through her head — thoughts about herself, what kind of a person she was, and how she felt about other people, particularly her parents and her grandfather. She didn't like what she came up with. I'm not a very nice person, she thought. I'm selfish and self-centered, but I'm going to try.

Josie tossed and turned and still could not fall asleep. She felt frightened and lonely, not at all convinced that a person could change herself. She thought about Michael. He was an enigma, and she wondered what he thought of her, an unsophisticated country girl. She stretched her body, feeling the marvelous strength of it, and tried to forget about growing old and dying.

Suddenly she jumped out of bed and crept down the stairs. It was stupid to fool Miss Laura or upset her. She'd do the dishes tonight.

Josie was surprised to find a light in the kitchen. And there was Michael standing at the sink. He gave her a startled look, and his face flushed. "I couldn't sleep, so I thought I might as well get these damned dishes out of the way."

Josie laughed. "Two minds with the same thought." She patted Michael on the shoulder. "I guess we both feel the same about Miss Laura."

"Cut it out," he growled and turned the faucets on full force.

$\mathcal{S}$even

As the summer days went by, Josie felt cut off from the life she had always known. Summer had been a time to be lazy, to go swimming, to sit on the green with her friends. But now it was running all day for Miss Laura — sometimes with Michael, sometimes alone — and taking her out for drives in the afternoon. There were days when she felt she couldn't stand it, that she had to get away, but there really was no place to get away to. She could never quite shake off Miss Laura.

When she had an afternoon off and spent time with her friends, Josie was not entirely at ease. They talked about things that she was no longer part of, and a corner of her mind was worried about whether Miss Laura was all right.

"It's like leaving a baby at home," her mother said. "I can't go out of this house without worrying whether Grandpa's going to be all right. But you have to go. You can't stay in all the time. You get too crotchety, and that's no good for anyone."

"Miss Laura's not my baby. I'm just working for her," Josie said. "She's not my problem."

"You feel responsible for someone old," her mother told her. "No matter how good they are and how much they can do for themselves, it ain't the same. They're slow; they can have accidents. You don't like to leave them alone."

"Yeah, I know." But what really troubled Josie were her feelings for Miss Laura. Sometimes she couldn't stand her. She hated her vanities and her demands and fussiness. But other times she came close to loving her because of her independence and humor. Although she had grown up with her aging grandfather in the house, Josie felt that she had never truly known anyone old. She had never paid any attention to her grandfather. Mainly he had been a source of irritation to her. But now she was seeing similiar characteristics in sophisticated, spoiled Miss Laura and her uneducated, farmer grandfather. They both wanted to hold on to life as they knew it, to their past, not to be displaced into something new and strange, even in their thoughts, and they both wanted to keep control of their affairs.

When Josie came home, she began to take a new interest in her grandfather. After all, she had his blood in her veins, and there he was living in the same house with her. She had never been curious about his life, his childhood, but now she stopped to talk to him when she had a chance. He responded wholeheartedly. He regaled her with stories about coming to America at the turn of the century, a small boy crossing the Atlantic in the steerage of a boat packed with immigrants. His father had had a cousin who lived in Hartford, and they had gone there, and then his father had worked on a tobacco farm. "We had nothing that you kids have today," he told her. "No electricity, no water in the house, no radio, no television, but we got along. We had our good times and our bad times. That's how it goes, Josie. One part of your life balances off another."

The day of the wedding was drawing near, and Josie was helping to plan the wedding breakfast. The ceremony was scheduled for eleven o'clock in the Polish Catholic church, and after the breakfast for the wedding party, there was to be a big dinner and reception for all the friends and relatives in the firehouse. "I guess they'll start coming to the firehouse around two, or before even, and they'll be coming and staying all day. I keep worrying there won't be enough food," Mrs. Smyrski said.

"Wedding shouldn't be in no firehouse. Should be at home," old man Smyrski said. "Folks stay and dance all night, and the next day and next night too. That's the way it was in the old days. Nobody wanted to go home after a wedding."

"If they don't want to go home, they can come back here," his daughter-in-law said. "But things are different now, Pop."

"Ain't so much fun neither," he grumbled.

"I'm going to bake a couple of extra hams, just in case," Mrs. Smyrski said.

"I thought you told me everyone was bringing food," Josie said.

"Yes, your Aunt Helen's making stuffed cabbage, and Marion Douskey's making the kielbasa, and someone's doing stuffed chickens, and there are my hams, and of course there'll be lots of salads, and nut cake, and cookies. Mary's friend, Mariano, the baker, is making her wedding cake."

"It sounds as if you have plenty," Josie said.

"Providing there's enough beer and wine," her grandfather offered.

"I'm still going to make some more hams," Mrs. Smyrski said determinedly.

When Josie told Miss Laura that she would need that Saturday off and why, Miss Laura's face lit up. "A wedding, how wonderful. May I come?"

"It's not going to be anything fancy, just a big Polish family wedding. I don't think you'd like it. . . ."

"But I'd love it. I've never been to a Polish wedding. Please ask your mother if I may come."

Laura felt uneasy. "It's nothing special. Just a lot of eating and drinking, some music and dancing."

"Sounds better all the time. Oh, please, please." Miss Laura was like a little girl.

"If she goes, I do too," Michael said. "I like weddings."

"I'll have to ask my mother."

Josie knew well that her mother would say, of course. Two extra would mean nothing to her. But Josie didn't think she liked the idea. She thought of the Van Dyks. What would they think of her taking Miss Laura to a family wedding? And she thought of some of her uncles who drank a lot of beer and told embarrassing stories, and her grandfather who slopped his food over his shirt. . . . The more she thought about it the more she hated the idea.

Then it occurred to Josie that she didn't have to ask her mother at all. She could simply tell Miss Laura no. The thought was a great relief, and she made up her mind that that was what she would do. It wasn't quite honest, but why in the world should an old lady like Miss Laura want to come to a wedding when she didn't even know the bride or the groom? It was just another silly notion of hers.

That day after lunch Miss Laura asked Josie to come up to her room. "I want you to help me pick out what I should wear to the wedding, although maybe I should get something new. When I was young, we always bought a new gown for a wedding. We'll take a look through my closet, although I'm sure there's nothing suitable." She giggled conspiratorially. "Henry says I'm too extravagant, but I do love new gowns, and I haven't been to a wedding in a long time."

Josie steeled herself. "I'm not sure about the wedding, Miss Laura. Like I told you, it's a family affair...."

"Of course my dear, a wedding always is. I'll be very quiet, and I won't eat much." She gave Josie one of her sudden, sly looks. "You tell them you're working for a balmy old lady, and you had to bring her along. No one will pay attention."

Josie sighed. She knew she was licked. When Miss Laura made up her mind to something, there was no changing it. Without much enthusiasm Josie hauled out long dresses under Miss Laura's direction. Miss Laura discarded one after another. She was sitting with a thoughtful expression on her face when she turned to Josie. "Not one is right. I should have a new gown anyway. This will probably be the last wedding I ever go to."

"Why do you say that? You'll go to loads of weddings," Josie said with forced gaiety.

Miss Laura shook her head. "No, my dear. No one lives forever, and I am very old. Getting older every day. I expect I'll die soon."

Josie was alarmed. "Don't say that. Are you all right? Do you feel all right?"

"Of course. I feel fine. But I have a premonition of death. Don't be alarmed. Dying is a natural process. It's nothing to be afraid of. Paul wasn't afraid to die. He died with great dignity, and that's what's important. Not to die squirming. I'd hate to do that." Miss Laura smiled at her brightly. "All of which makes me think I should buy a new gown."

"You don't really need one. Not for this wedding."

"Don't deprive me. You see, my dear, when you know you are going to die soon, you want every minute of your life to count. And it's never too soon to think that way. You never know. . . ."

Everything the old woman said should have made Josie feel depressed, she thought, but strangely enough she was not. Miss Laura looked so calm and content that she made death seem as natural and simple as the leaves falling from the trees in autumn. "Make every day of your life meaningful," Miss Laura said.

"I don't know how," Josie told her.

"Then you'd better learn. I didn't accomplish much. I wasn't a great artist like my husband. I didn't go around doing good deeds, but I had great joys. I experienced everything that came my way. That was what made life meaningful for me. You have to find your own way."

"I'd like to be an artist, to paint," Josie said.

"Then be one. Simply do it. Start right here and now. Do it for your own pleasure. You can go down to Paul's studio and work there every day for a couple of hours. Don't even let me stop you. I can respect that, although I may forget about it and call for you."

"Would you really let me use your husband's studio?"

"I wouldn't say so if I didn't mean it. Here, I trust you with the key and not to disturb anything of his. Go down now, while I take a rest. We'll go shopping tomorrow."

Josie sat in the large studio with the north light streaming through the great skylights, in awe of her surroundings. She didn't know where to start, what to do. Miss Laura had told her there were drawing pads and pencils, charcoal, canvases, paints — whatever she needed or wanted she would find there. "There's no sense saving all those things," Miss Laura had said. "I think Paul would like a girl like you to use them." Josie was overwhelmed. She felt that there was nothing that she could do that could possibly match the gift of such a place to work in. She felt tiny and inadequate. Then an idea started taking shape in her head. Miss Laura had once said to her, "Of course technique is important, but Paul always had something he wanted to say in his work. Talent and skill are one thing, but the statement of the artist is what makes something a work of art."

Josie thought about her grandfather. She decided that she wanted to make a drawing of him. She didn't need to have him sit for her. She knew his face well, and she didn't care if it was an exact likeness. She wanted to try to express her feelings about him in a drawing; she wanted to get the stubborn pride in his face, his humor, the stamp of age and his aloneness when he sat in his chair on the porch with the faraway look in his eyes. It was not going to be a tender or sentimental drawing of an old man. He would hate that, and it wasn't the way she felt about him. She wanted to show him strong, with that bit of the tyrant in him that made him difficult.

Josie found a drawing pad and a soft pencil and started her sketch. She worked steadily, totally engrossed in what she was doing, forgetting her surroundings. She had never been so excited about anything she had done, ever. The time flew by, and she was surprised when there was a knock on the door, and she realized she had been working for over two hours.

Josie answered, and Michael walked in. Hastily Josie turned her drawing pad face down.

"What are you doing in here?" he asked.

"Miss Laura said I could work here."

"Can I see?" He reached for the pad.

Josie grabbed it first. "No. It's not finished. Besides I don't like showing it."

"What's the sense of drawing or painting for yourself alone?"

"What's wrong with doing it for myself? That's what Miss Laura said I should do. I enjoy it."

Michael gave her a curious glance. "You should have an audience." Then he looked at all the paintings stacked around the walls. "What's she hanging on to all these paintings for? Must be a fortune here."

"She loves them. She likes to look at them."

"But she ought to show them. Paul loved his shows. He once told me that the opening of a show was always the most exciting time of his life. What's going to happen to them when she dies?"

"You'll probably inherit them," Josie said. "Isn't that what you expect? You and your parents?"

"Don't mix me up with my parents. We think differently. That aunt of mine is someone special, and I'd like to see her end up with a splash. I told you before, I'm on her side. You know what I think? I think she should have a big retrospective show for Paul. Let her have the fun of it and the money too. Otherwise, it'll only go to my parents or me. It would give her something to be excited about."

"Would your parents let her do it?"

"I don't think they could stop her. She has the paintings, and all the good galleries in New York are dying to show them." Michael's eyes were bright with excitement. "I could help her with the arrangements. I'm going to talk to her this afternoon, as soon as she gets up."

Josie studied his face. "Are you doing this for your aunt or to spite your parents?" she asked bluntly.

Michael grinned. "Mostly for my aunt, but maybe a little for the other too. Anyway, I'd be cutting off my own inheritance too, wouldn't I? And it would be great for Laura."

"Yes, it would," Josie agreed. "But didn't your father say that your uncle wanted him to take care of any business to do with the paintings?"

"This wouldn't lose anything for Aunt Laura. A gallery will get good money for them, and Aunt Laura should have the fun of it. What can my father do? I think Uncle Paul was afraid that Aunt Laura might get gypped or give too many paintings away. But if she deals with a legitimate gallery, he can't stop her. He may get mad because she's doing it on her own without consulting him, and he may try to interfere, but that's all. I just hope he keeps out of it and doesn't spoil it for her."

Josie was beginning to like Michael. She had been suspicious of him and, she had to admit to herself, unsure of an older, sophisticated boy from New York. She hadn't been able to forget that she was after all only a hired girl working for his aunt. But his frankness with her was disarming, and she saw him now as a person with problems not entirely different from her own — both of them trying to figure out what they wanted to do — and with a true affection for his aunt. She wondered what he thought of her: Was she just a country kid to him or did he see her as someone attractive, interesting? Nuts, she thought, he probably had lots of pretty, glamorous girls in New York. But sometimes she wondered if he would have wanted to stay so long with his aunt alone.

Eight

Miss Laura was not as enthusiastic about a show of her husband's paintings as Michael had expected. "I don't know," she said. "I have to think about it. I like having them here. I like to look at them. It keeps Paul close to me. Besides, I'm afraid."

"What are you afraid of?" Michael asked.

She looked around as though to make sure that no one but Josie was there listening. "Those people. The people who want to take them away from me. How do I know you're not one of them?" she asked suspiciously.

Michael's face fell. Miss Laura was drifting away. Neither of them could get used to her abrupt changes from lucidity to confusion. "I'm Michael, your nephew," he pleaded. "I don't want to do you any harm. This would be for your good. Think of a gala opening, all your and Paul's old friends coming to a champagne party at a top galery. The press, the critics — it would be an important event in the art world."

Miss Laura's face brightened. "Maybe you have something. I must think it out. I don't want to be rushed into anything."

"There's plenty of time," Michael said.

"Now, Josie," she said abruptly, dismissing something she didn't want to think about, "we must talk about the wedding and what to wear. . . ."

Going shopping with Miss Laura was no easy task, as Josie discovered. Whatever she saw, regardless of the size or appropriateness, she wanted to try on, and then she made a terrible fuss about having to do so.

"She's impossible," Michael said. Foolishly, and much to his disgust after an hour and a half in one store, he had come along.

There was nothing to do, Josie decided, but to make a decision herself. "That blue dress is just right," she said firmly. "That's the one you have to have."

"Do you really think it's becoming? I'm not sure about the neckline." Miss Laura was looking at a purple shift a young girl had in her hand. "Maybe something like that."

"I don't think so," Josie said, warning Michael with a look not to laugh. "It's the blue. We'll take that. You'll look beautiful in it."

Josie sighed with relief when they were all back in the car with the dress in a box.

Josie wanted to be home getting herself ready for the wedding, but instead there she was helping Miss Laura to get dressed. And her patience was running out. Miss Laura had changed her shoes four times before she decided that the black pumps were the best. "I don't think my hair looks right," Miss Laura was saying. "It needs more fullness on the top."

"It looks okay," Josie said.

Miss Laura eyed herself critically. "It doesn't look okay. Don't tell me it does when it doesn't."

"What difference does it make?" Josie asked impatiently.

Miss Laura glared at her. "I have always been very fussy about my hair, and I do not intend to change now."

"Yes, Miss Laura." Josie wanted to yell, "Who do you think's going to be looking at you, you vain old thing?" but she controlled herself. And when she saw Miss Laura examining her wrinkles in the mirror she felt contrite.

"I used to have such beautiful skin and hair," Miss Laura said sadly. "I suppose you think I'm a silly old woman, and I guess I am, but I always like to look my best."

"You look lovely," Josie told her.

Josie went home to get dressed, leaving Michael to bring himself and Miss Laura to the church. Much to her surprise, cars and trucks were lined up outside her house, and the house and lawn were overflowing with people. The men were already at the kegs of beer standing outside the back porch. Josie ran inside to find her mother.

Mrs. Smyrski and Josie's aunts and cousins were in the kitchen. "What's going on?" Josie asked, seeing her mother's distraught face. "I thought everything was going to be at the firehouse."

"It is, but you know our family. They all came here anyway, and they're going to come back here after the reception, just like Grandpa said. You know how Poles are about a wedding."

"But what about the breakfast? They can't all come here for that?"

"There isn't going to be any breakfast. We'll go straight to the firehouse from church."

"What about Mary? Does she care?"

"She's too excited. Go upstairs. She's in my room getting dressed. I'm all confused about whether to take more food to the firehouse or to leave all this here for later. I think there's enough over there already, but I don't know. . . ."

Josie eyed the mounds of food spread out on all the space available. "You have enough here for an army."

"We have an army to feed," her mother said resignedly.

Josie ran upstairs to the bride. Mary's two sisters, in their petticoats, their bridesmaid's dresses spread out on the bed, were helping Mary. "Oh, Josie" — Mary put out her arms and hugged her cousin — "I'm so nervous. I don't think I can live through this day."

"You'll make it," Josie said. "Look out, you'll crush your dress." She stood back to survey Mary in her long, full bridal gown. "You look absolutely beautiful!"

"You put on my veil," Mary begged.

"Of course."

With the younger girls helping, Josie adjusted the fine lace veil that had been Mary's mother's. Mary was almost in tears. "I wish Mother was here," she said sadly.

"We all do," Josie said.

"But your mother's marvelous. I don't know what I'd do without Aunt Lena."

"I'd better go get dressed," Josie said.

In her own room Josie felt an unexpected sense of warmth and security. The room was tiny compared

to the one she slept in at Miss Laura's, and her bed
was a plain, old bed she'd had all her life instead of
an antique four-poster, but the feeling of being home
was good. She liked hearing the bustle of the women
downstairs and the laughter of the men outdoors.
This was her family, and they were warm and loving
and made her feel comfortable. It was also a relief to
know that for a little while she would not hear Miss
Laura's plaintive voice calling, "Josie, Josie."

When she got away from Miss Laura, she realized the strain on her demands and her own irritation with them. Taking care of an old person meant
being on an emotional seesaw, first irritation and
then guilt. Maybe, Josie thought, there were old
people who were beautiful, wise, self-sufficient, the
kind of people authors wrote sentimental stories
about, but Josie doubted that any of those authors
had ever lived with one. Even her grandfather, who
took care of himself, acted as if he had a right to say
what he pleased and to demand what he wanted.
And yet, Josie reasoned (easier to do when she
wasn't at Miss Laura's beck and call), it could be
that if old people didn't make themselves heard,
didn't demand attention, they were too apt to be
ignored. That was something to think about.

Josie dressed herself quickly in her pale-yellow
bridesmaid's dress and then went back to the bride.
"You look absolutely beautiful," she said to Mary
again, and couldn't help admiring her own reflection
in the glass too. This wedding had come at just the
right moment for Josie. Being with people her own
age again refreshed her spirits, and she felt, she
hoped, that when she went back to Miss Laura's
she would be less irritated and impatient.

Josie and Mary's two sisters got into the car with

Mary and her father to drive to the church, but most of the other relatives walked. John, the groom, would drive from his own house with his best man. The church was beautifully decorated with fresh flowers, and Josie thought she must be almost as excited as the bride. The wait for the ceremony to begin seemed interminable. It was almost noon before everyone was assembled and ready. At last the organ started to play, and the wedding procession started. Josie kept her eyes downward as she walked down the aisle, fearful of tripping on her long dress, but out of the corner of her eye she spotted Miss Laura's white head and Michael's dark one. They both looked odd to her sitting among her country relatives, and she turned her eyes away quickly, afraid that she might giggle.

The solemn, sacred ceremony went off smoothly except that the best man, John's brother, almost dropped the ring as he handed it to the groom, and again Josie had to control her desire to giggle. After the bride and groom had been pronounced man and wife and kissed each other, the family and friends gathered around with a great deal of kissing and hugging.

Josie finally tore herself away and saw Miss Laura and Michael standing off by themselves. She went to them and found Miss Laura in tears. "I always cry at weddings," she said, wiping her eyes. "Even strangers. It was beautiful. Just beautiful."

"Don't cry. You're supposed to be happy at a wedding. I have to stay until the pictures of the wedding party are taken, but you and Michael can go over to the firehouse. Michael can drive, or do you want to walk?"

"I can walk," Miss Laura said firmly.

Josie wished with all her heart that Miss Laura had not insisted on coming. She wanted to be free to be with her cousins and aunts and uncles, many of whom she hadn't seen for some time. She didn't want to have Miss Laura on her mind. "Take her home early," she whispered to Michael. "She'll get tired soon anyway."

"Don't whisper, you two," Miss Laura said sharply. "I'm looking forward to this," she added. "I expect to have a very good time." She spoke as if she knew, with her instinctive shrewdness, that they were plotting to deprive her of her fun.

Josie joined the bridal party in an anteroom to pose for the photographer. In the meantime, her mother and aunts and friends hurried over to the firehouse to see that the long tables were all set up and the food set out so that the seated midday dinner could be served. An orchestra would also be there, waiting for the arrival of the wedding party to begin the music.

When all the pictures had been taken, Josie went to the firehouse with the other attendants while John drove his bride to the hall. They were greeted with the band playing the Polish wedding march, and Josie's mother, taking the place of Mary's own mother, approached the young couple and offered them salt and bread: the bread so that they might never know hunger, and the salt so that wealth, health, and happiness would be theirs for many years.

What everyone called the firehouse was actually a separate building alongside the garage that held the fire engines and town ambulance. It was a large, rectangular, one-story, red-brick structure that the Volunteer Firemen had erected to use for their annual country fair that they also made available for local affairs. Now it was a gay scene with festive decorations, people dressed in their best finery seated at the long tables, and the young girls of the family serving the dinner from a huge serving table laden with food: the traditional stuffed cabbage, kielbasa, roast stuffed chicken, slices of ham, pork loins, and sauerkraut, cold cuts, salads of all kinds, coleslaw, pickles, rolls and butter, cakes, and cookies. The centerpiece of the table was the wedding cake. Wine and beer flowed freely, and, for the children, there was soda. While everyone ate, the orchestra played lively Polish tunes: polkas, mazurkas, obereks, and waltzes. When it was time for the wedding cake to be cut, the bride and groom together cut the first slice, and then portions of the cake were passed around before the nut cake and cookies and coffee were served. There were many toasts to the young bride and groom.

Josie kept leaving her place with the bridal party to go over to Miss Laura and Michael to make sure that they were being taken care of. "I'm having a taste of everything there is," Miss Laura announced. "I don't want to leave one thing out."

"Just be careful you don't get sick," Josie warned. Then in a whispered aside to Michael, "I feel like her mother."

"I've never felt better," Miss Laura said. Her blue eyes were sparkling, and she was obviously enjoying herself.

After a while the tables were pushed to one side along the walls to clear the room for dancing. The bride and groom were to dance first, but before they did, someone called out, "Throw your bouquet, Mary, throw your bouquet."

In minutes all the single young girls collected

around the bride. The bride closed her eyes and threw her bouquet over her head, into the outstretched arms of a very pretty dark-haired girl. "Now it's your turn, John," Mary said to him.

"Why is everyone laughing?" Miss Laura asked. She had insisted on coming with Josie to see what was going on.

"You'll see," Josie told her.

John picked up his bride's long skirt and took off the blue garter she was wearing below her knee. Then he closed his eyes and tossed it over his shoulder to the group of single young men who had gathered around. There was a howl of glee when the garter was caught by a pudgy boy of about fifteen. The boy's face was crimson as, amid a loud round of applause, he put the garter on the leg of the girl who had caught the bouquet. Miss Laura was ecstatic. "Oh, they're adorable, simply adorable. . . ."

Josie was somewhat embarrassed by Miss Laura's loud enthusiasm and wondered if she was going to tag alongside her all afternoon. But members of the family were coming up to introduce themselves, and Miss Laura greeted them all charmingly. After Josie took her back to her seat, Miss Laura sat tapping her foot to the rhythm of the music, her eyes moving around the hall so as not to miss a thing. She kept asking for more wine and was still nibbling on a cookie she had in her hand.

"Now what's going to happen?" Miss Laura wanted to know.

Josie's mother was unpinning the bride's veil. She removed it and shaped it into a cap and placed it on the table. "That's for wedding gifts of money," Josie explained. "Most relatives like to give a young couple money. Mary got lots of other things for her house at the showers that were given for her, and there are more presents back at our house." Even as she spoke they saw envelopes being dropped in the veil. "Also there's an old custom of men paying to dance with the bride. My mother doesn't approve of it, but I think a lot of the men will do it anyway."

"I think it's a fine idea," Miss Laura said. "Why shouldn't they pay to dance with a pretty, young bride?"

The bride and groom danced together first, and then the hall resounded with the thump of many feet as almost everybody joined in. Michael and Josie became breathless doing a polka, until, exhausted, Josie sank down on a chair next to Miss Laura.

"How about a waltz with me?" Michael asked his aunt, when the music struck up again.

"I've been waiting for you to ask me," she told him with a mischievous smile, and off they glided.

Whatever hope Josie had of Miss Laura's getting tired was soon dashed. As Josie's mother kept saying, "She's the life of the party." Miss Laura drank all the wine that was poured for her. She talked to everyone, and when old Mr. Smyrski came over to ask her to dance, everyone stood around in a circle and clapped. Their polka was not as vigorous as the young people's had been, but they put on a good show. Josie was afraid that Misss Laura would have a heart attack, but everytime Josie tried to get her to sit quietly for a little or to let Michael take her home, Miss Laura refused. "I'm having the best time I've had in years, and you're not going to stop me."

Josie looked to Michael for help, but he, too, refused. "She's enjoying herself, so why spoil it? If she has a heart attack, she'll have one. She could probably have one sitting at home."

"I don't want her to have one here when she's our guest," Josie said. She kept thinking about what the Van Dyks would say if they saw Miss Laura prancing around with an old Polish farmer, and then she thought, Why not, if they're enjoying themselves? After a while Miss Laura sat down next to her grandfather, and when Josie walked near them, she could hear them happily reminiscing about the old days. She thought it odd that elegant Miss Laura and her grandfather should be friends, but the sight of them together gave her a good feeling.

The music, the dancing, and the drinking went on until late in the evening. The farmers who had to take care of their animals went home to do barn chores and then came back. Even the bride and groom did not leave, but stayed on dancing with all their friends and relatives until they looked as if they might drop on the floor. Josie couldn't get Miss Laura to leave. She had given up dancing, but she sat in her chair, wide awake and alert, and would not budge. "I'll leave when the honeymoon couple leave," she insisted, "and not before."

Josie sighed with relief when at last Mary and John said good-bye to everyone and took off in John's car in a shower of rice and a blowing of horns. Josie knew that all the guests who were still there were going to adjourn to her parents' house and keep up their merrymaking all night, and probably well into Sunday, but she didn't dare tell Miss Laura that. Miss Laura, she decided, had had more than enough of a Polish wedding. Josie herself was exhausted and ready to get Miss Laura to bed and to go to bed herself. But when they got to the house, Miss Laura said that she wanted to go to the studio.

"What on earth do you want to do there now?" Josie asked. "It's late, and we're all tired."

"You may be tired, but I'm fine," Miss Laura said contemptuously.

Michael laughed. "You two can fight it out. I'm going to bed."

"Come on," Josie pleaded.

"No, I've got to take care of this now while it's on my mind. I'm going to pick out a nice picture for that pretty bride. Paul would like me to give her a present, I'm sure."

"You can't give her one of your husband's paintings. You don't even know her. Please, Miss Laura."

"Of course I know her. I went to her wedding, didn't I?"

Miss Laura marched into the studio, and Josie could do nothing but follow. Miss Laura knew exactly the painting that she wanted to give to the young couple. She directed Josie to pull out a good-sized oil landscape of a rural wooded scene. It was painted in rich autumn colors that would light up and grace any room it was in. "There, that's the one. Do you think they'll like it?"

"Anyone would love it," Josie said. "But you can't give it to them. It's too valuable. Your brother-in-law would be very angry." She realized immediately that she had said the wrong thing.

"What do I care about making him angry! None of his business what I do. The idea . . . ! I can give any painting away I want to. I don't need his permission. We'll take that over to the framer's Monday. Put it in the dining room so we won't forget. That's the right picture, I know it is."

Josie took the painting out as Miss Laura asked, but she was worried. She supposed she ought to call Mr. Van Dyk, although she felt that then she would be betraying Miss Laura, and so Josie went to bed with a troubled mind.

Josie's worry did not disappear overnight. In the morning she was still trying to decide whether she should call Mr. Van Dyk or not. She asked Michael what to do. Michael thought her question was funny. "Listen, if she wants to give someone a wedding present, it's her affair. Why shouldn't she? She had the best time yesterday she's probably had in a long time. It's worth it to her."

"But the painting's probably worth thousands of dollars. Your father told me to call him. I feel responsible." Josie hadn't really expected much help from Michael, although she was rather glad to see him on Miss Laura's side. Still, she had a forlorn hope that since Michael was family he would take responsibility for Miss Laura's giving the painting away.

"If you think I'm going to call him, forget it. I don't want to have anything to do with the whole thing. As you've told me many times, you're the one who has the job here. You do what you think you ought to. I can only give you my opinion, and I think my aunt has a right to do what she wants."

"I think so, too," Josie said, but she was still troubled. Then she decided that she was working for Miss Laura and no one else and that she wasn't going to act as some kind of informer, although she did have a wistful thought that maybe Miss Laura would forget about the painting.

But no such luck. Miss Laura looked at it the minute she came downstairs. "A very simple frame," she said. "Paul was very fussy about frames. He always said that most framers wanted to outshine the picture."

On Monday Miss Laura was in her element at the framer's shop. There was no hesitation or indecision. She knew exactly what she wanted and gave the framer explicit directions. Josie couldn't believe she was the same woman who kept losing her pocketbook or her glasses or her checkbook, or made inappropriate remarks. She wished the Van Dyks could see her now.

Miss Laura's good spirits held on the drive home. "Your grandfather is a very interesting man," she said to Josie. "He knows a great deal about animals. We must ask him over to tea one afternoon."

Josie giggled. She couldn't picture her grandfather coming to Miss Laura's to tea. "I don't think he's much of a tea drinker."

"Then we'll give him a glass of sherry."

That sounded just as funny to Josie. "He doesn't go out much."

"Well, he should. You mustn't discourage him. He's an old man, and we must be nice to him." Miss Laura spoke as if she were many years his junior. "He likes people, I can tell, and he shouldn't be alone all the time."

"When you want him, I'll ask him," Josie said, still amused at the thought of her grandfather and Miss Laura having a tea party.

Nine

Miss Laura did not forget that she wanted to invite old Mr. Smyrski to tea, and she insisted that Josie ask him. Much to Josie's surprise, her grandfather accepted readily. "A nice woman," he said. "Talks too much, but she ain't stupid."

Josie felt strange when she went to call for her grandfather. He was dressed in his best suit and a clean shirt, and there was a twinkle in his eyes. "Stepping out in society I am." She had borrowed Miss Laura's car to get him. Her mother had her parents' car at work, and her grandfather had said it wasn't proper to call on "a grand lady" in her father's truck.

If ever there was an unlikely pair, Josie thought, it was those two. When she brought Mr. Smyrski into Miss Laura's sitting room, and he sat down in front of the fireplace next to Miss Laura, she realized with astonishment that Miss Laura was flirting with him.

"They're adorable," Josie whispered to Michael, after she had left the two of them alone. "Absolutely incredible." Her grandfather had expanded in a way she had never seen, asking Miss Laura about her travels and telling her about his impressions of New York when he had first landed there.

He was more knowledgeable than she had ever given him credit for, and when he got on to the subject of Miss Laura's house in Jacob's Brook, which he had seen enlarged and remodeled over the years, she was entranced.

"Who would think those two old people would have so much to say to each other?" Josie said to Michael.

"I guess old people have feelings like everyone else. Aunt Laura always was a flirt and could turn on the charm when she wanted," Michael said.

"I don't know. I keep changing my mind," Josie said musingly. "Sometimes I could murder your aunt, and at other times she's adorable. My grandfather, too. I'm really trying to be nicer to him and to get to know him better, but sometimes he makes me want to scream. I don't know how my parents put up with him. They've had him, and my grandmother too before she died, ever since the day they got married. Not for me. If I ever get married, I sure don't want my parents to live with me."

"I don't want to live with my parents even before I get married," Michael said wryly. "It's a problem. I told you, the only solution is not to get old. Let everyone die at sixty."

Josie grimaced. "That's a lousy idea. Actually I suppose anyone can bug you sometimes, young or old. We pay too much attention to age. I get tired of being called a teen-ager, and I guess old people get tired of being called old. Right now, though, I'd better see what the odd couple are doing."

Her grandfather was just getting up to leave, and Miss Laura was flushed and pretty as she saw Mr. Smyrski to the door. Josie's grandfather was in high spirits when she took him home. "I had to live to be eighty-five to go and drink tea with a lady," he said with great amusement.

Miss Laura was still bouncy at dinner that evening, and Michael decided it was a good time to bring up his idea of a show of Paul's paintings again. Miss Laura was still reluctant to agree. "I just hate to part with any of them," she said, repeating what she'd said before.

"But you don't really look at them that often," Michael argued. "They're just stacked in the studio. This way you'd have the fun and excitement of a show, and you'd have the money. Otherwise, well. . . ." He didn't want to say they wouldn't do her any good after she was gone.

Miss Laura gave him a piercing look. "Otherwise, what? I know what you're thinking. What will happen to them after I am dead? Don't be afraid to speak of death to me, Michael. I know very well I am going to die, and it doesn't upset me one bit. Death is not a bad word, and the way everyone goes around speaking about it in hushed tones is ridiculous. It's part of nature, just as being born is."

"All right, Aunt Laura. So what will happen to them after you die? They'll be disposed of, and you won't be here to enjoy the result. I think you're being silly about them."

Miss Laura laughed. "Imagine my nephew calling me silly. Paul did love having a show. He was as excited as an actor on opening night. It would be very strange to have one without him. I just don't know. . . ."

"I think Uncle Paul would approve," Michael said. "He wouldn't like all his paintings kept where no one can see them. Think of that."

"I do think of that. I'm always thinking of what Paul would do or say. I suppose you're right, Michael. I'm a bit of a fool keeping his work shut up here. Why not have a show? It would be exciting. . . ." Her eyes brightened. "All right. There's no sense mulling about it any longer. Once I make up my mind that's it. You get that gallery man up here, Michael. We'll have a dinner party, the way we used to, to plan the show. Paul was a better businessman than Henry ever believed. He knew how to get people excited about a show. We gave lots of dinner parties and invited museum people and the big collectors and even some of the critics, if they were friendly. Paul liked to plan all the details of a show, and he also liked to get everyone talking about it. What'll we have for dinner, Michael? You want to make Paul's veal dish?"

"Sure, why not? I'm game, if you help and tell me what to do."

"We can have some cold salmon first, and no soup. We don't need soup. Then the veal, tiny potatoes, artichoke hearts, and a green salad. What'll we have for dessert?"

"Something light," Michael suggested. "How about a chocolate mousse?"

"Sounds divine. Do you know how to make it?"

"It's one of my specialties," Michael told her.

"I hope I'll be invited," Josie said. "I've never eaten any of those things before."

"We wouldn't dream of not having you, my dear," Miss Laura said.

"Who are you going to invite, Aunt Laura?" Michael asked.

"That's the big question. I'll have to give it a lot of thought. In the art world you have to be careful not to bring two people together who are ready to knife each other. I want to ask Ephram Levy — he lives up here someplace and is a big collector — and that nice woman from the National Academy, I always forget her name, some museum people. . . . The idea is to mix money and professionals. But not too many. We never liked to give dinner parties for more than twelve or fourteen. I *am* excited." Then her bright face saddened. "How Paul would love this. I can't get used to the idea of having a show without Paul." She picked up the cat, Heloise, who had been snooping around the table. "But maybe Paul knows," she whispered to the sleek cat.

Michael was elated, but Josie was worried. After Miss Laura had gone to bed, she sat down to talk to Michael. "You and I can't go ahead and help her have a big show without your parents knowing about it. I have to tell them."

"But it's none of their business," Michael argued.

"Yes, it is. This involves thousands and thousands of dollars, and you and I won't know whether she's doing the right thing or not, or whether she's getting gypped. We know she can be sharp, but she also goes off, too. I will not take that responsibility. It would be crazy."

"You don't trust her. That's the trouble."

"I guess it is," Josie agreed. "She's very old, and she's not always rational. You know your parents may be right in wanting to protect her. And your father did say Paul had given him a letter asking him to take care of the paintings for her."

"Protect her from what?" Michael demanded. "Paul is dead, and Aunt Laura is alive. My father is exaggerating the importance of that letter. I saw it when Uncle Paul died. It actually only asked my father not to let Aunt Laura get gypped. She laughed about it and said Uncle Paul was always overprotecting her. My father's reading a lot into it. She won't get gypped. The paintings belong to her, and she has a right to do what she wants. What if the paintings did bring in more money five or ten years from now? She'd be dead. I'm the one who would eventually inherit her money, and if I don't care, why should they?"

Josie had never seen Michael so vehement or so serious. He was very different from the aimless boy she had first met, the boy who seemed to be out for himself. "You've certainly changed. What makes you so generous all of a sudden?" Josie was still not sure of him.

Michael sensed her wariness and got angry. "So I've changed. What's so wrong with that? I've done a lot of thinking since I've been up here, and I think my aunt's terrific. Maybe she does go off her rocker sometimes. That doesn't mean she should be treated like a half-wit and pushed around. There'd be no point in even having a show if my father took over. It's not for the money; it's for what it would mean to Aunt Laura. If she made a thousand instead of a hundred thousand, it would be worth it."

"But she needs money. She can't pay her bills," Josie protested.

"She'll pay them eventually," Michael said. "Besides, the paintings aren't doing her any good sitting in the studio. Whatever she makes, and believe me she'll make a lot, will be so much extra. But it's putting on the show that counts."

"I don't know, I just don't know." Josie was torn about what to do. In principle she agreed with Michael. Miss Laura should be able to do what she wanted, and yet she felt responsible to Mr. Van Dyk, too. She and Michael were just kids, and Mr. Van Dyk was Paul's only brother and executor of his will. Paul must have put some value on his judgment. What if the art show was a flop, or if it did make the money Michael thought it would, what if Miss Laura frittered all of it away? The truth was that she was more involved with Miss Laura than she had ever thought she would be or wanted to be. Instead of working for a senile old woman, she had found a person with vitality and a strong hold on life in spite of an old body and a wandering mind.

The next afternoon Josie went home, and for the first time in her life that she could remember, she decided to ask her parents for advice. Her grandfather was sitting in the kitchen, too, when she explained the situation to her mother and father. Old Mr. Smyrski was the one who spoke up first. "Don't you go letting anyone interfere with that old lady. She knows what she wants. She ain't stupid or crazy. Like me, if I wanted to sell off my land and throw my money into the garbage pail, it ain't nobody's business but mine. People's feelings is more important than money. She'd be proud to show off her husband's pictures, and she likes parties and all that fol-de-rol. Me, I like to look at my fields, and I don't care if nobody else sees them. But if she wants to sell them pictures, she's got a right to."

"Your grandfather is right," Josie's mother said.

Her father, however, wasn't sure that he agreed. "The girl's got a responsibility. If the family don't want her to do this, and Mr. Van Dyk asked her to let him know, she's got to do it. It ain't right for her to do something like this on her own."

"Nuts," her grandfather said bluntly. "She don't owe nothing to Mr. whatever his name is. He did wrong asking her to spy on the old lady. Josie ain't a jailer. Mr. Whoosis, he's the one who made a mistake."

Josie listened to her family argue about her problem, and she became more and more convinced that her grandfather and her mother were right. Her grandfather, in a way, made the most sense. After all, Mr. Van Dyk had no real right to interfere and ask her to keep a watch on Miss Laura. "If he really wanted to help the old lady," her grandfather said, "he'd want to make her happy, let her do what she wants instead of treating her like she's got no mind of her own." That cinched it for Josie. She put her arms around the old man and told him that she was glad to be able to talk things over with him.

"Any time," Mr. Smyrski said grandly, "any time, I'd be pleased to help you out."

She had to smile at how pleased he was with himself, but she was genuinely happy for his advice. Michael wasn't the only one whose attitudes had changed, she thought.

At the moment Miss Laura was more excited about her dinner party than she was about the art show. For two days straight she had Josie making and tearing up lists for guests. Josie thought she would go crazy if Miss Laura changed her mind one more time. "Fourteen people sounds just right," she pleaded with Miss Laura, as she saw that wavering look in her eyes.

"Well . . . maybe. I started out with ten, but

now I'm sure there are some important people I'm forgetting. What happened to that list we made yesterday?"

"You told me to tear it up. You said it would be confusing to save it."

Miss Laura looked exasperated. "That's ridiculous. I never said such a thing. Never tear up a list. You don't know when you might need it. Now I forget who was on it."

"The same people you have on this one, except that you added two more. Fourteen seems a very good number."

Miss Laura glared at her. "My dear child, the number of people at a dinner party is not important, it's who they are."

Josie kept quiet. It was one of those days when she could say nothing right.

Getting Miss Laura to settle finally on a menu was even more difficult than the list of guests. She had already forgotten what she had told Michael. Mrs. Thompson threw up her hands in disgust and complained to Josie. "That old woman is balmy. She gives me a bunch of French names I ain't never heard of. I'm going to make her a nice roast capon, roast potatoes, a green vegetable, and a salad. It'll be a real nice dinner and none of her highfalutin' fancy sauces. Only make people sick anyway."

Unfortunately, Miss Laura heard her and rushed into the kitchen. "If you think you're going to cook one of your church suppers for my dinner party, you're mistaken. I'm not that balmy — a vulgar word — that I still don't know good food or how to give a dinner party. I will give you a menu," she said to Mrs. Thompson and flounced out of the kitchen.

"Old biddy," Mrs. Thompson muttered.

Michael was the one who finally got his aunt to settle on a menu, and Josie helped him persuade Mrs. Thompson that he was capable of doing a great deal of the cooking. "What you young kids doing all this for? Expect her to remember you in her will?"

"We're doing it because we like her," Michael said.

"Mmmph," Mrs. Thompson snorted. "Who can like a balmy old lady like that one!"

Josie was amazed by her anger. "Damn it, everyone has it in for old people."

"Your parents don't," Michael reminded her.

"Maybe it's because they're more European. Their whole attitude is different."

Josie and Michael were determined to see that Miss Laura had a beautiful dinner party. Josie sent out the invitations, and Michael contacted the owner of the gallery, who was most enthusiastic about having a show of Paul Van Dyk's paintings.

For days before, amid Mrs. Thompson's grumblings, the house was a scene of cleaning, polishing silver, freshening table linen, baking, and cooking. The day of the party Josie was up early, a list in her hand of all the things that she had to do. There were Miss Laura's clothes to get ready, flowers to be picked and arranged, the table to be set, wine to be chilled. Josie had never handled anything like this before in her life, and she was both excited and nervous.

The guests were invited for seven o'clock, and at around five thirty, just as Josie came out of the shower, a car pulled into the driveway. Much to her horror, she saw Henry and Celia Van Dyk walking to the door, Mr. Van Dyk carrying a suitcase. She threw on a robe and ran out of her room calling for Michael. The Van Dyks had definitely not been on the guest list, and the thought flashed across Josie's mind that their arrival might not be a coincidence. That meant trouble, big trouble.

Michael was already downstairs, as upset as she was. "It's just not a good time to come for a visit," he was saying to his parents. "Why didn't you call first?"

His father wasn't paying much attention to him. Instead he was talking to Mrs. Thompson. "Please set two more places at the dinner table. You can put Mr. Gallagher, the gallery man, next to me if you would, please. We'll use Mr. Paul's old room, and I think Mrs. Van Dyk would like a cup of tea now, please."

"Yes, of course," Mrs. Thompson said. "And it's a good thing you've arrived what with the goings-on around here."

"That's exactly why we came," Mr. Van Dyk said.

"You came to spoil everything," Michael yelled at his father. "Who told you about this anyway?"

Mr. Van Dyk was furious, and to Josie that made him more human than did his usual cool facade. "Michael, you stay out of this. I have to remind you again that I am the executor of my brother's will. His paintings haven't been inventoried, no prices put on them. Gallagher may be an honest man — he called me up assuming I knew about this show and this dinner party — but I have to watch out for her interest. Laura doesn't know what she's doing. The whole thing is crazy."

"It's not crazy," Michael persisted. "The paintings are Aunt Laura's, and she ought to be able to do what she wants. You're concerned about the money. I'm thinking of her. Planning this show has made her young again, and that's what counts."

"It's not up to you to decide. You and this girl here are meddling into something you don't know a damned thing about. Yes, I am concerned about the money. An art show of Paul's paintings is big business, and I'll be damned if I'll let an old woman handle it. I owe that much to my dead brother. He asked me to protect her."

"Protect her from what? From being a person instead of a nothing. You're not doing what Uncle Paul would want. You're doing what you want! It's not fair; it just isn't fair," Michael yelled. "Why can't you leave her alone?"

"Because I have a responsibility, that's why. I don't want to discuss it any further."

"No, of course not. You care more about money than you do for a person. She may be old, but she still has feelings, and her mind's damn good."

Mr. Van Dyk picked up his suitcase and went upstairs without answering his son.

Josie, who had been standing on the stairs listening to the conversation, now flew back to her room before Mr. Van Dyk came up. In a few minutes there was a knock on her door, and she let Michael in.

"You tell her," Michael said.

"Not on your life," Josie said. "I'm staying out of this. It's your family, between you and your parents."

"That makes it worse." He sat down on the

edge of her bed, his chin cupped in his hands. "Why can't people leave other people alone?"

"They think we're meddling."

"But we're not. We're just letting an old woman run her own affairs. It isn't as if she was really senile; it's money. My father worries so damn much about the money. If the paintings weren't worth anything, he wouldn't care. Kids and old people are in the same boat," he added glumly.

"Kids don't have money," Josie said.

"That's what I mean. They're dependents. That's why they get pushed around. And it's the same with old people. If they have money, someone wants to get it, and if they don't, they're out of luck, too."

"Well, what are we going to do?"

Michael shrugged. "Nothing, I guess. We'll just have to see what happens."

As expected, when Miss Laura discovered that her in-laws had arrived, she flew into a rage. Josie was scared because the poor woman was quite incoherent. She mixed up events that had happened in the past with what was happening now, and Henry was talking to her as if she were a baby.

Celia Van Dyk stood by looking white and helpless. "You just don't understand your father," she said to Michael. "He feels responsible. He's doing what he believes is his duty, that's all. I know you and your father don't get along. You see things differently, but don't be too hard on him, Mikey. I know he can't accept you, but you're young. Try and take him for what he is. He's not going to change."

"But Aunt Laura was fine until you came along. Now she's upset and confused. You don't know the fantastic time she's been having planning the party. Now it's spoiled."

"What can I do?" Celia was close to tears. "It's terrible when people in a family don't get along, the way it used to be with Henry and Paul and Laura. But now Henry thinks he's helping. You've got to believe that, Michael."

"I don't think I can. He doesn't trust me. Why should I trust him? The difference is that I love Aunt Laura, and he doesn't. And Aunt Laura needs love, not someone who's doing his duty. It's that simple."

"You make it sound simple, but I'm afraid it's more complicated. Oh, dear. . . ." She put her arms around Michael and for a minute or two sobbed on his shoulder. "It's an awful thing to say, but sometimes I wish Laura would die. I can't stand all this worry and squabbling."

Michael patted his mother, but his eyes, as he looked over her head at Josie, were determined. "Don't you get yourself so upset," he said to his mother. "You have to believe that Josie and I care for Aunt Laura, and we think we're doing what's right for her."

Henry finally persuaded Josie to give Miss Laura one of her pills to quiet her down. Josie agreed reluctantly and watched her wilt with a sinking heart. This was to be her big night, and now Josie saw her turn from a proud woman with life and dignity into a worn, old woman, disoriented and submissive. Josie knew it wasn't just the tranquilizer. Miss Laura felt her inability to match strength with her brother-in-law. "They're too much for me," she muttered. Then she asked in a plaintive voice, "Is Paul fixing the drinks? Paul is famous for his martinis. . . ."

"Paul isn't here," Michael said to her gently.

"Tell him to hurry up if he's still dressing. He should welcome our guests. I'm very tired."

Josie served at the table while Michael helped Mrs. Thompson in the kitchen. The atmosphere was everything Josie had dreamed of when she had imagined how the beautiful people lived in their beautiful houses: gleaming silver and china, soft candles, flowers, sparkling wines, fashionable men and women talking brightly, laughing at each other's witticisms. It was almost like that — almost, if not for the tired old woman at the head of the table. Her guests talked around her and past her, giving her an indulgent smile every so often, pretending that everything was all right, but in the midst of their chatter exchanging sorrowful glances. "Poor Laura Van Dyk, how old and sad she's become. . . ."

Josie wanted to scream at them, "She doesn't have to be that way. She could have been as bright as any of you tonight if she'd been given a chance, but she's been robbed of her right to make some decisions for herself." Josie hated them all, hated them for not helping Miss Laura, for not really talking to her, for acting as if she didn't exist, wasn't their hostess. How could people be so cruel as to sit as guest at someone's dinner table and not even try to draw her out? Instead, they let her sit there dabbling at her food, looking sad and bewildered, while they laughed and joked around her.

Josie was still furious when, even before the coffee was served in the living room, she heard Henry Van Dyk say to his sister-in-law, "You look very tired, my dear. We'll excuse you if you want to go upstairs to bed."

113

"I *am* tired," she said. "I think I will go."

Josie went upstairs with her and wanted to enfold the old woman in her arms. "It was a beautiful dinner party," she said. "Everything was lovely."

"Yes, it was." Miss Laura spoke in a faraway voice. "But it wasn't the kind we used to have when Paul was alive." Josie felt relieved, but also saddened. Miss Laura was oriented to reality once again, but her reality was sorrowful. "People have changed," Miss Laura said. "They're not friendly anymore. They're all so busy talking about themselves. No one even asked me how I spend my time." Josie felt as though these were the saddest words she had ever heard in her whole life.

Miss Laura patted Josie's arm. "You did everything very well, my dear. It wasn't your fault that the party wasn't a success."

"It was a lovely party," Josie said, wanting to console her.

"I guess I'm too old for parties," Miss Laura spoke with resignation, and Josie wished she had gotten angry instead, but all spirit seemed to have left her.

When Josie went downstairs to help clean up, she saw Henry Van Dyk and the gallery man through the partly open door to the library, engaged in serious conversation. Undoubtedly they were arranging between them the details of the art show, if there was going to be an art show. Josie felt sick at heart.

Josie went to bed that night feeling that somehow she had failed Miss Laura. She didn't know what she could have done, but the nagging feeling persisted as she dropped off to sleep.

Ten

The next morning the house was very quiet when Josie woke up. It was almost too quiet, and Josie jumped out of bed to peek into Miss Laura's room. She was still sound asleep, undoubtedly still tired from the night before. Michael was also still sleeping, but when Josie came downstairs the Van Dyks were in the kitchen, dressed to leave, having some coffee. Their suitcase was already in the hall.

Josie was greeted with a cool good-morning. "My sister-in-law must be very tired if she's still sleeping," Mr. Van Dyk said. "She's usually such an early bird. I knew last night was too much for her."

"She had really looked forward to the evening," Josie told him. "I think she was upset."

"Of course she was upset, poor dear," Celia Van Dyk said, shaking her head and looking unhappy. "All this is too much for her. She's too old and frail for so much excitement. She should be someplace where she has a calm routine."

"If you don't mind my saying so, I don't think she'd be very happy that way." Josie did not look at either one of them but busied herself making a fried egg.

"We're thinking of her health," Mr. Van Dyk said briskly.

Josie had to control herself. She wanted to point out that Miss Laura's health was okay if they'd leave her alone. Her state of mind was upset but nothing else. She was dying to ask if the art show was still on, and if so, when it was going to be, but she didn't dare.

"Are you going to wait for Laura to get up?" Mrs. Van Dyk asked her husband.

"I'd like to talk to her, but I have to get to my office." He turned to Josie. "We're very opposed to an art show just now. We think it will be too much for Miss Laura. The paintings can remain where they are for the present. You could help persuade her to drop the idea of the show, if you would."

Josie was immediately on guard. "I don't think I could, sir. She has her heart set on it now. I — we thought it would be good for her, give her something to do, to think about."

"By 'we' you mean my son and yourself. You two children are taking a lot on yourselves, dealing with things you know nothing about. It's quite outrageous. If I had my way, my sister-in-law would be in a rest home where she'd be properly taken care of."

Josie was shocked by his anger and frustration. There was nothing cool about him now, even his hand was trembling as he lifted his coffee cup. She almost felt sorry for him, because she realized that there was nothing he could do. He couldn't fire her, and he obviously had no control over his own son. She was also a little frightened. What if she and Michael were doing something harmful for Miss Laura? Yet all her instincts told her that they weren't. She knew they were right. Even her grandfather had told her that. Thinking about her grandfather gave strength to her conviction: If anyone tried to run his life for him, treating him like an incompetent, he'd either have a heart attack or fold up into a broken man.

Josie didn't answer Mr. Van Dyk and hoped that he and his wife would leave before Miss Laura got up. Fortunately they did, without saying good-bye either to Miss Laura or to Michael.

Michael came downstairs first, and he sighed with relief when he heard that his parents had left. "I hate to admit it, but the less I see of them right now the better. Maybe someday we'll be able to communicate. I don't know when. I'm afraid my staying here with Aunt Laura doesn't help matters any, but I think its good for her, and I'm enjoying it. Besides," he added with a wry smile, "I haven't any place else to go."

"I wonder what happened about the art show," Josie said. "They didn't say a word, and of course I didn't ask them."

"I hope they didn't call it off. We'll see when Aunt Laura gets up."

When Miss Laura did get up, she said that she had no idea of what had happened and that she had never gotten to talk to Mr. Gallagher at all. "It's that damn pill he insisted on. It was a superb dinner, Michael, and I hope there are some leftovers, because I didn't eat much last night. I'm starving now."

"But what about the art show?" Michael insisted.

"After I eat," his aunt said, peering into the refrigerator, her main interest at the moment being food.

* * *

By the end of that day Josie was exhausted, and her head was in a whirl. She had literally spent all the afternoon getting either Henry Van Dyk or Mr. Gallagher on the phone for Miss Laura, listening to Miss Laura scream with rage, worrying herself sick that something awful was going to happen to her or scolding Michael for egging her on. Mr. Gallagher had started the whole thing off when he assured Miss Laura that he was as eager to have a show of Paul's paintings as she was but that he had been given to understand that he was to deal directly with Henry Van Dyk. At that point, Miss Laura had stated that not a painting was leaving her house under conditions invented by a stupid idiot and that they could all go to hell. After Michael had calmed her down, she then called Henry and gave him a strong taste of her feelings about his arrival the night before and about his interference. Afterward there were more telephone calls back and forth than Josie could count, and all she could think of was that she hoped Miss Laura would have the money to pay the telephone bill. By the time they went to bed, Josie thought that there was going to be an art show if nothing happened the next day to change things again, and that Miss Laura was almost satisfied that no one was going to put anything over on her.

Michael said, "You know, Aunt Laura, my parents are not mean people. I don't happen to agree with them, but from their point of view they honestly think they're acting for your good. Even Uncle Paul used to say that neither one of you was businesslike."

Miss Laura snorted. "Of course they're not mean. But God help me from the Henrys who think they're doing their duty, and poor Celia just trots behind him. I think I'm old enough to take care of myself," she added with a wicked smile.

Weeks of planning and discussing went by, and the art show was a reality. The opening was going to be the next afternoon. Josie had propped on her bureau the announcement and the small enclosed invitation to the select opening reception. She had to keep looking at it to make sure it was for real. She had lived through every one of its nerve-wracking stages: Miss Laura tearing up proofs declaring they were the cheapest-looking things she'd ever seen, changing the wording, wanting a different painting of Paul's reproduced on the cover of the four-page brochure, and nearly on several occasions calling the whole thing off. Josie had come to dread any communication from the gallery, but she had also learned something about timing. Although she felt devious at first, she learned to hold the mail from her employer until the right moment, usually when Miss Laura was having her glass of sherry before dinner. Then the mood was more mellow, and she couldn't rush to the phone to call the gallery because it would be closed. By the next morning there would be a good chance that Miss Laura's agitation would have calmed down. Michael assured Josie that she was not being devious but, on the contrary, becoming sensible in dealing with his aunt.

But Josie was not looking forward to the day. Getting Miss Laura ready for the trip to New York the following afternoon was going to be a monumental production. Yet, as Josie was getting dressed, she thought back on the summer and realized how much better she was now at coping. The job had

119

been a stopgap arrangement for her, but not only had she developed a strong affection for Miss Laura, she had learned a lot about herself. The preparation for the art show had made clear to her what she had suspected all summer, ever since she had come to Miss Laura's. She was not dedicated to becoming an artist. She still liked to draw and to paint for pleasure, but she did not have the ability to work concentratedly and consistently, nor the drive to make a long, uphill struggle like Paul Van Dyk's. Strangely, she was not depressed by this knowledge. In a way she felt freer, knowing that she wasn't going to strive for a impossible goal. Living with Miss Laura had made her feel strong, and good about herself, less of a nonentity; she *was* helping Miss Laura, and some of Miss Laura's strength had rubbed off on her.

"Josie, Josie. . . ." Miss Laura's voice interrupted her thoughts.

"I'll be with you in a minute," Josie called back. She knew what would be awaiting her. Another hassle about what Miss Laura would wear to the opening, a worry about her hair, another harangue about her brother-in-law — it was all familiar ground by now.

By lunchtime practically everything in Miss Laura's closet had been brought out for inspection and many choices made and changed. Finally a black suit was decided upon, and Josie kept her fingers crossed that the decision would stick until the next day. As for Miss Laura's hair, Josie was able to persuade her to go to a beauty parlor to have it set. "I loathe beauty parlors," Miss Laura said, "but if you say so, I'll go. They'd better do what I tell them, though, and not what they want to do."

After supper, when Miss Laura was safely tucked into bed, Josie heaved a sigh of relief. "I'll be glad when this is over," she said to Michael. "I only hope it's not going to be too much for her. I get scared that your parents may be right."

"Nuts," Michael told her. "This is her life, and she should have it. As I've said right along, putting her on the shelf is keeping her only half alive."

"I know, but I still get nervous."

Although Josie lived about a hundred miles from New York, she had been to the city only twice in her life: once when the graduation class from elementary school went on a sightseeing trip, and another time when she went with her class to the planetarium. She was both excited by the city and frightened of it, and when Michael parked Miss Laura's car at a garage and she walked with him and Miss Laura to the gallery in the East Sixties, she clung to Miss Laura's arm. She would have loved to stop to look at all the shop windows, and Miss Laura told her that she could meet them at the gallery, but she said that she wouldn't go off alone for a million dollars.

Michael teased her and called her a hick as she looked up at the tall buildings and stared at all the people and the cars. "I'm just not used to it," Josie told him. "It's bigger than New Haven or Hartford. Those are the only cities I really know."

They arrived at the gallery before the guests were due to arrive. Only Celia and Henry Van Dyk were there, besides the gallery people. Celia greeted her son effusively and bent down and kissed Miss Laura. "It's a beautiful show," she whispered.

"Of course it is," Miss Laura said tartly. "Don't you think so, Henry?"

"Of course," Mr. Van Dyk said, but he did not kiss his sister-in-law, Josie noticed, nor give her or Michael much of a greeting. Josie only hoped that he would not spoil the day for Miss Laura.

Josie tried to persuade Miss Laura to sit down and rest for a while, but she couldn't wait to walk around to look at her husband's paintings. Josie walked around the gallery with her, holding her arm. They stopped before each painting for a long while, and at times Josie could feel Miss Laura's whole body tremble. Obviously this was a moving experience for her. In front of one painting, of her self many years before, sitting in a boat with a large straw hat on her head, Miss Laura laughed heartily. "Oh, what a time we had that day. It must be fifty, sixty years ago. Paul insisted on going out in that ridiculous old boat, and I was terrified. As usual, he had his drawing pad with him, and when he started to sketch I got furious. I wanted to go back to shore, but not Paul. He had started an idea for a painting, and I could yell my head off, but he wouldn't leave until he had what he wanted. I used to say I hated that painting, but I really never did. It's lovely, isn't it?"

Josie thought all the paintings were beautiful, and when Miss Laura asked her which was her favorite, she couldn't make up her mind.

The reception was to begin at five o'clock, and by five thirty the gallery was jammed. There was practically no place to move around, and it was impossible to get near the long table where at one end wine and cheeses were being served. "Nobody's looking at the pictures," Josie whispered to Michael. "They're all just talking to each other."

"That's what always happens at an opening. If they want to see the pictures, they have to come back another time."

Miss Laura, however, was in her element. Perched on a high-backed chair, she sat like a queen, condescending to smile and chat with those who came to pay their respects, but, as Josie noticed, giving some a cool greeting. With one very old friend of Paul's, a distinguished white-haired man, she almost broke down and wept. Tearfully they hugged and kissed each other. The crowd in the gallery didn't begin to thin out until around eight o'clock, and by that time Miss Laura was visibly tired. But she refused to leave until the last guest had departed. "It's been a beautiful day for me," she said with a sigh. "Sad, too, because Paul wasn't here, but I felt him close to me all the time."

There was much discussion with the Van Dyks as to whether Miss Laura should stay in the city overnight or drive back to the country. Miss Laura settled the question herself, emphatically. "I am going home. I have no desire to sleep in someone else's bed, and all this talk is absurd, Henry."

Josie was very relieved when Miss Laura and Michael and she were all in the car and on their way home to Jacob's Brook.

Eleven

Josie was in a deep sleep when she woke to Miss Laura's voice calling, "Help, help, Josie, Josie. . . ." In a second she was out of bed and running into Miss Laura's room. Miss Laura was half out of bed, clutching at her chest and gasping. "Terrible pain . . . I want to get up but I can't. . . ." Miss Laura's face was deadly pale and she was breathing with difficulty.

Josie was terrified. She lifted Miss Laura back onto the bed and tried to quiet her. "I'll get help. Can you lie quietly for a minute or two?"

Josie ran to the hall calling for Michael, but he was already there, tying his robe around him. Michael took charge. "Josie, call the hospital and get an ambulance here fast. Tell them to have an oxygen tank. She's having a heart attack."

Michael was beside Miss Laura's bedside, kneeling down, giving her mouth-to-mouth resuscitation while Josie stood by. Josie thought the ambulance was taking forever, although by the clock it was at the house in less than ten minutes. She and Michael watched while the ambulance attendants gave Miss Laura some oxygen to ease her breathing and then gently lifted her onto the stretcher. "Josie," she said faintly. "Can Josie come with me?"

"I'm here, I'm right beside you," Josie said to her and looked inquiringly at the attendants. "May I ride in the ambulance with her?"

"Yes, sure."

"I'll follow in the car. I'm going to get some clothes on," Michael said.

Josie had never ridden in an ambulance in her life, and she was both scared and excited riding through the night at breakneck speed with the wailing siren going. She held on to Miss Laura's hand, feeling as if somehow she could pass some of her strength into Miss Laura's body.

At the hospital a doctor was waiting in the emergency room, and Josie was shut out in the waiting room. She had pulled on a pair of jeans and a sweater, but she found herself shivering. Michael arrived and sat beside her on the hard bench. Neither of them spoke, and every once in a while Michael took her hand and patted it. Josie kept thinking of what was going on behind the closed door and wondering if Miss Laura was going to die. She found it hard to conceive of death. Was it just going to sleep and not waking up, or was your soul transported into some unknown world? Although Josie did not believe in life after death, the absence of all life and thought was hard to imagine. Maybe when you got old and tired it was nice to rest quietly and peacefully, not to have to think. . . .

After a while Michael got up and began pacing up and down the room. He made Josie nervous, but she didn't say anything. She wondered if he was thinking the same thing that she was: if they hadn't pushed her into putting on Paul's art show, would this have happened? She couldn't bear to think about it — it was too painful a thought — and she couldn't possibly talk to Michael about it now.

She wanted to concentrate on Miss Laura, and she didn't want any interference. If she concentrated hard enough, Miss Laura would be all right. Finally the doctor came out and spoke to them in low tones. Miss Laura had had a coronary, and they were taking her up to the intensive-care unit. They would know more in the next day or two. "We've relieved the intense pain," the doctor said, "and she is quite alert considering her age. She can have no visitors. Perhaps one member of the family can see her tomorrow for a few minutes."

"May she say who?" Michael asked.

"I don't know why not," the doctor said.

"Could I go in to see her now for just a minute?" Josie asked.

The doctor peered at her over his glasses. "Are you the girl who rode in the ambulance with her?" Josie nodded. "You can run in and see her for exactly one minute before she goes upstairs," the doctor told her.

Josie followed him into the emergency room. Miss Laura looked small and frail and white, flat on her back with a sheet draped over her, but her eyes opened to meet Josie's, and Josie knew that she recognized her. Josie took one of her hands, squeezed it, and whispered, "You're going to be all right." Miss Laura's eyes acknowledged the words.

The next few days were a nightmare for Josie. She couldn't believe that the sun was shining brightly and that there was the exhilarating, brisk feeling of autumn in the air. Miss Laura's garden was ablaze with the yellow and orange of late-blooming flowers: zinnias, marigolds, dahlias, and chrysanthemums. Some of the trees were beginning to turn into bright shades of red and yellow, a sure sign of winter ahead. Mr. and Mrs. Van Dyk had arrived that first day and were staying with them.

Josie was able to take no pleasure in the fine weather. Her mind was torn between anxiety and guilt that she and Michael were to blame for Miss Laura's heart attack, and she was deeply concerned for Miss Laura herself. "Your father was right," she said to Michael. "If we hadn't had that damn art show, this never would have happened."

"How do we know?" Michael reasoned with her. "She could have had a heart attack anytime. I'm glad she had the show. It was a tremendous experience for her."

At home, Josie wept, and her grandfather tried to comfort her. "Don't blame yourself. You have to live, especially when you're old. Every day counts, and if that old woman enjoyed her husband's art show, then it was good she had it. Having no fun when you're old ain't no good. You got to take some chances. Young fellers get hit with heart attacks too. She could have got one sitting home in her chair."

Living side by side with the Van Dyks in Miss Laura's house was almost unbearable. Josie felt their accusing eyes on her constantly, and she wasn't quite sure why she remained. Without Miss Laura there to be taken care of, she could have gone home, but Michael begged her to stay, and in a way she didn't want to leave. She had an eerie feeling that if she left, something dreadful would happen and that somehow her presence was important for Miss Laura. She and Michael never spoke about it, but she sensed that he felt the same way, that they both had to be there, not only for Miss Laura but to give each other moral support.

Josie spent a good deal of her time at the hospital, waiting to be told when she could have a few minutes with Miss Laura. Henry Van Dyk hated her, she knew, because Miss Laura wanted to see her and no one else. Celia Van Dyk was her usual weak, apologizing self, trying ineffectually to keep some peace between her husband and her son. The doctors were making no commitments. Miss Laura could pull through or she could go at anytime; there was no way of knowing, they said.

Miss Laura had been in the intensive-care unit almost a week when Henry Van Dyk told Josie they didn't need her and she could leave. There was no point in paying her salary anymore.

"I don't care about the salary," Josie said, "if I can be useful."

"There's nothing we need you for," he said, and Michael's intervention was of no avail.

That night Josie went up to her room with the big four-poster and tried to sort out her thoughts. Miss Laura had hired her, and she wasn't sure that someone else had the right to fire her. And when she saw Miss Laura at the hospital, Miss Laura seemed to take for granted that she was at the house waiting for her to come home. She asked about the garden and the cat and who had called. She never spoke much, and sometimes her mind wandered and she sent home messages to Paul and said she knew he was busy painting and that's why he couldn't come to see her. Josie felt she would be betraying Miss Laura's trust by leaving but she didn't know how to stay. She was oppressed by the feeling that getting rid of her was a first step in getting rid of Miss Laura.

The next morning Josie gathered up her courage and faced Mr. Van Dyk. "Miss Laura hired me," she said, "and I think it's up to her to tell me to go. I think she wants me here."

"My sister-in-law is in no position to make decisions now," he said curtly.

"A heart attack hasn't changed her. She's still the same person."

"I see no reason to discuss the matter any further. I appreciate your loyalty to Miss Laura, but I think I know best."

Josie felt that she was up against a stone wall. There was nothing to do but to pack up her clothes and go home. Michael drove her over to her house, and the two of them sat in the car in her driveway talking gloomily.

"They're going to put her in a nursing home," Michael said.

"Maybe she'll be better off," Josie said, not believing it for a minute.

"She'll hate it. A nursing home may be fine for some people, especially if there's no other way, but she has a home that she loves. Even if you couldn't stay, they could get someone to live with her. My father doesn't want her to handle her affairs, that's all, and my mother leaves it up to him. Also, my mother says it's too hard to find the right help. They think you're too young."

"There's nothing we can do about it," Josie said resignedly. "Why do people do things like this?"

"I don't know. My parents aren't bad people;

they just don't have any sensitivity. My father thinks in business terms — protection of property and crap like that. He really believes that he's protecting Aunt Laura from running through her money. He doesn't know how to leave her alone. He's thinking of property instead of a person."

"I'm glad my parents don't feel that way about my grandfather," Josie said.

Only her grandfather was home when Josie went inside. Her mother was at work and her father was out. "Too bad about the old lady," her grandfather said. "But maybe she'll be lucky."

"Lucky how?"

"Go fast. That's the way. Live slow, drag out every minute for what it's worth, and die fast."

"Do you want to die fast?"

"You bet your life. Everyone talks about death in whispers. They make a whole rigamarole out of dying when it's just as natural as living. Ain't nothing mysterious about it. The worst thing is living miserable. Those the people I feel sorry for. If you live good, dying ain't nothing to cry about."

"But it's so final, so like nothing," Josie said. She had never had a conversation like this with her grandfather.

He chuckled. "By golly girl, that's what's good. When you get old, it ain't bad to lie down and rest."

"I hope I can feel that way when I get old," Josie said admiringly.

Her grandfather looked up at her from his chair, and his eyes held a lot of tenderness. "You got my blood in your veins, Josie, good strong blood. You live good, and you won't mind getting old, and you won't mind dying when the time comes. Just don't spend your life worrying about it like a lot of people do. They worry so about dying they don't enjoy living. People live a long time now, and if you make every day count, it adds up to a lot of good days."

Josie put her arms around her grandfather and gave him a kiss. "I'm glad I've got your blood in my veins," she said. "It makes me feel strong."

Josie went to the hospital every day to see Miss Laura. After about two weeks in intensive care she was moved to her own room in the hospital and was able to have more visitors. While she still looked very frail, the doctors were optimistic about her. Yet Josie thought her face was sad and that she had aged considerably more than just a couple of weeks.

Josie tried to see her when no one else was there, and Miss Laura talked about going home. She took for granted that Josie was still living in her house. "Get Michael to put up the storm windows before you turn on the furnace, and get the furnace man to clean the furnace." Josie marveled at her memory for details, although her mind wandered in other areas. At times she mixed up the art show with shows that had taken place when Paul was alive. But very often she spoke about it with a glow of pleasure. "Thank God we had that show before I got sick," she said to Josie many times. "You and Michael did it. It was your idea, and I'll always be thankful to you both. It's a good thing we had it before this silly heart of mine kicked up." Her words gave Josie great comfort.

Miss Laura's thoughts were always on going

home. "The food here is awful," she said. "When I get home, we're going to have lots of parties and good food. The only meal that's fit to eat here is breakfast. They cover the meats with greasy gravy that I can't stand."

When Josie called at Miss Laura's house to tell Michael about the storm windows, she found Mrs. Van Dyk making an inventory of all the furnishings. "What's going on?" she asked Michael.

"You know what's going on. They're going to put Aunt Laura into a nursing home, and I guess they'll get her to sign whatever papers they need to sell the house. That's what."

"Can't you stop them?"

"What can I do? They think they're doing the right thing. They won't take you back here; they say you're too young. Besides, you wouldn't do it anyway, would you?"

Josie couldn't answer him. Even though she knew the question was academic, part of her wanted to say, yes, of course I will, but there were too many things pulling her in other directions. She was only seventeen, she thought. Miss Laura was not her relative. She had her own life to live, and living with Miss Laura had been something to do only for the summer. She hadn't expected to get so involved.

"I love Miss Laura," she said to Michael, "but she should live with her family."

"She hasn't got a family to live with," Michael said bluntly.

"I know." Josie sighed. "The whole situation is awful. I don't know the answer, but there's something wrong about it. I hope by the time we get old they'll figure out a better way."

"Who's they?" Michael asked.

Josie laughed. "Us, I guess. I hope we figure out how to get old without being pushed around."

Josie went to see Miss Laura at the hospital often and listened to her make plans for going home, which Josie knew was not going to happen. Then one day Michael told her that Miss Laura was going to leave the hospital for a nursing home. Josie had known that was coming, but she was still shaken by it.

"Have you told her yet?" she asked Michael.

"The doctor told her. He told her that she needed more care than she could get at home. She was her usual fantastic self. She cursed him out thoroughly, told him he didn't know his business. She really let him have it, the nurse told me. When I saw her, she had calmed down. At first she was terribly depressed, but then she perked up again. I have a feeling she'll turn that nursing home inside out. She's something."

"I'll have to go up and say good-bye to her." Josie did not look forward to that.

"Yes, you'd better. She'll be in New York, but you can go to see her there."

"It won't be the same." Josie looked up at Michael. "What about you? What are you going to do?"

"I think I'm going to try to get into a good cooking school. What about you?"

"I haven't decided. Maybe try for a job. When you open up a restaurant, let me know. I'll come and eat your soufflés."

Michael grinned. "It's been a good summer, Josie. Let me know if you ever come to the city."

"Yes, I will."

They had been standing on the hospital steps, and Josie watched him walk away. Their bond had really been Miss Laura, living with her and taking care of her, and with that gone she doubted that she would ever see Michael again. The thought made her sad; everything seemed to be coming to an end. She dreaded going up to say good-bye to Miss Laura, but resolutely she went into the hospital.

Miss Laura was sitting up in bed looking at a television program, which she turned off when she saw Josie. "Have you heard the news? They're shipping me off to a nursing home. *Nursing home*, the two most hated words in the English language."

"You might like it there," Josie said, without much conviction.

"I doubt it. But you know what? I screamed and yelled, and then I decided I didn't care. I'm tired, Josie, too tired to fight anymore. I've had a good life, I have good memories, and I can take them with me anywhere. No one can take them away from me."

"Of course, Miss Laura. You're a wonderful woman. I hope I'm like you when I get old."

"Enjoy your life, child, and you'll stay young. Young in spirit that is, and that's what counts."

Josie stayed with Miss Laura for a little while until she saw that she was getting tired. When she left, she decided not to say good-bye. She bent down and kissed Miss Laura and said, "Take care. I'll come see you in your new home one of these days."

"Of course you will," Miss Laura said. "But come soon. I may not be there very long." There was no fear or self-pity in her voice. Her matter-of-fact tone and her somewhat wry smile made Josie ashamed of her own depression.

Twelve

The lawn in front of Josie's house was covered with leaves. She sat on the porch with her grandfather watching them fall. Heloise was curled up on her lap. Michael had asked her if she wanted the cat, and Josie had taken her happily. She loved Heloise and had made Michael promise to tell his aunt that she would be the best cared-for cat in the world. "It's as if I'll have something of Miss Laura's with me," Josie had said.

The October sun was warm enough for her to be comfortable in her jeans and a shirt, but her grandfather was bundled up in a heavy sweater with a scarf around his neck. "I used to love winter," Mr. Smyrski said. "We went sleigh riding, your grandmother and I. We never minded the snow, but now I dread the cold."

"You stay nice and warm," Josie said.

Her grandfather gave a long sigh. "I'm never warm. From September to June, I feel cold. I guess my blood ain't what it used to be. . . . What are you going to do with yourself now, Josie? You can't sit around here all winter."

"Where can I go?"

135

"I dunno. That's up to you. But you got to get out of here. There ain't no future for you here."

Josie looked at her grandfather in surprise. "I thought you liked me to be home. Are you kicking me out?"

The old man laughed. "Yep. I've been thinking things over. I'm gonna sell a couple of them lots, and you can go to school. I don't need all that land. Why wait till I die?"

Josie was stunned. The thing she'd been wanting so badly for such a long time should make her feel ecstatic. But it didn't. She was touched, yet sad. "No, don't do that. I don't want you to sell any land for me. If I want to go to school I'll figure out a way. I've given up wanting art school anyway. I'm not a real artist."

Her grandfather didn't say anything for a long while. Then he murmured, "You're a good girl, Josie. A chip off the old block."

Josie didn't know what she wanted to do. When her friend Debbie had come home, she had felt that they had grown miles apart. Debbie had been full of her summer of parties and swimming and beach picnics. Tales of another world they seemed to Josie. "What did you do? Did you have any fun?" Debbie asked her.

"I don't know if you'd call it fun. I stayed with Laura Van Dyk, took care of her I guess you'd say."

"How could you stand it? Is that all you did?"

"Not much else," Josie said. "It wasn't bad. I . . . oh, well, never mind."

"What were you going to say?" Debbie demanded.

"Nothing," Josie said. She couldn't have begun to tell Debbie about her summer. How could she explain to anyone that spending a summer with an old lady had given her much to *think* about, had changed her feelings about things that mattered, like family and people, and how to live and how to die. . . ?

Those were strange days for Josie. She walked across her grandfather's fields and sometimes just sat under a tree and looked up at the sky. Often she walked past Miss Laura's house. She didn't know why, because it made her feel sad to see it look so uninhabited. Then a *For Sale* sign was put in front of the house. Sometimes she walked up into the garden and sat in it and picked off the dead flowers.

One day she was sitting in the garden when she heard voices from in back of the house. She went to see who was there and discovered two boys from the village trying to jimmy open a window.

"Hey, you, stop that," she yelled at them.

The kids, probably twelve or thirteen years old, looked at her in surprise. "We ain't doin' anything," one of them said. "Just wanted to see what it looks like inside."

"You're not going to. Get away from there or I'll brain you," Josie said.

"What's it to you? It ain't your house. What you doin' here anyway?"

"None of your business. The lady who lives here is a friend of mine, and you are not going to break in."

"You can't stop us," the older of the two said. "We're not going to steal anything."

"I'd like to believe you. But you get away, or I'll call the police."

The boys laughed. "You wouldn't do that. We're just having a little fun. Ain't no one living here, and the old lady's nuts anyhow. They've taken her away to the nut house."

"They have not," Josie said fiercely. "This is her house, and you just leave it alone." She picked up a rock. "I'll throw this at you if you don't go away."

"You're nuts. You look crazy." The smaller boy made a face at her, but he turned away, and the older one followed. Halfway down the driveway they turned around and threw some stones at Josie, but the stones fell at her feet.

When the boys left, she sat down and cried. They were tears of anger, anger at the unfairness of the world, anger at people's inhumanity. After a while she stopped crying and realized that she was exhausted but that she felt better. Miss Laura would have gotten a laugh out of seeing her holding a rock to throw at the boys. If she had thrown it, she probably would have hit a window instead. To laugh was part of the way Miss Laura and her grandfather said to live — to enjoy, cry sometimes of course, but to make every minute, every day count — and she'd been going around moping like a droopy petunia.

That night she announced at the supper table that she was going to New York to look for a job. When she had enough money, she might go on with her schooling. Her mother looked worried and her father said, "You're a country girl, Josie. You won't like the city."

"Let her find out for herself," her grandfather said. "She's got to live her own life. But don't forget,

Josie, if you run out of money there are a couple of lots down by the road we can sell off."

Josie shook her head. "Thanks a lot, Grandpa, but I'll make out. Listen, if you made it here from Poland when you were a kid, I guess I can make it to the city okay. After all, I've got your blood in my veins." She gave him an admiring and grateful smile. "I hope I make out as well as you did. I don't need any handouts, but thanks anyway."

"I ain't worried," her grandfather said. "Lena, you don't make sausage the way Grandma did. It ain't as tasty as hers, needs more seasoning in it."

"Same old Grandpa, telling everyone what to do," Josie teased him, but her eyes were tender and affectionate. "I got a present for you," she said, remembering the drawing she had made of him.

When she brought it down from her room, her grandfather looked at it critically. "Not bad, not bad for a beginner," he said, squinting his eyes. "Don't look exactly like me — nose too big — but not bad. What you want to draw an old man like me for anyway?"

Josie looked at him and at the picture. "Maybe I like old people," she said. "Even when they're impossible, they've got something. Maybe it's all those years they've lived," she added and blew her grandfather a kiss.

out that Miss Laura's health was okay if they'd leave her alone. Her state of mind was upset but nothing else, she was dying to ask if she are anyone